MEN OF HONOR

NEW YORK TIMES BESTSELLING AUTHOR

STEPHANIE TYLER

WRITING AS

SE JAKES

MEN OF HONOR, BOOK 5

They can't deny the attraction...or the danger...

Since losing their beloved third to cancer, Keith Masters and Johnny Lou Reed haven't thought about filling the void in their lives with anyone else. Until a stormy Christmas Eve, when a half-frozen, newly discharged Army Ranger shows up on their doorstep—with no memory of who he is or how he gotthere.

The former Marine in Keith is suspicious that he can't turn up any information about Shane anywhere, not even an address. Direct questioning will have to wait until they've gotten the boy well.

Shane knows it's only a matter of time before Keith and Reed figure out his past. And when they learn the depth and the darkness of the secrets he holds, he could get them all killed.

In the heat of the dark winter nights, the three men discover a passion that heals the gaping wounds in their hearts. And Shane wonders, despite the danger hot on his heels, how he will ever bear to leave...

Warning: Contains secrets, undercover operations
and three hot, alpha military men
who can set a cold winter night on fire.

Always for the readers...
thank you!!!

1

Shane wasn't sure how far he'd walked after the trucker dropped him off. At some point, the rain had turned to hail that sleeted in diagonal sheets and stung his face as he attempted to push farther along to find the motel.

"Two miles," the trucker had said. "I'm late, or else I'd take you."

He'd just shrugged and headed into the diner for some coffee and food before making this leg of the trip. No cabs in this weather, and with little money, the choice between food and transportation seemed obvious. He was young, strong and had his own twofeet.

In the Army, he'd walked through sandstorms and artillery fire, carried men through hell to get to safety. Frostbite didn't concern him.

He'd been numb for the last five months anyway. He'd been forced to leave his job—his life—behind. Lost a love he'd never thought he'd find there anyway, had a killer on his six and tried to convince himself that all of this was his punishment for getting Kyle killed.

Now, he realized that walking through this storm wasn't the best idea he'd ever had. Not when he was feeling sick on top of the fractured ribs he'd gotten hours earlier, both of which made breathing difficult. He was barely cognizant of what state he was in, although if he had to guess, upstate New York during one of the worst storms in years, if he'd heard the incessant weather reports correctly during his more wakeful hours.

The fever that had been dogging him for weeks seemed to decide that right now was the perfect time to hit him full force.

Yeah, Shane had enough troubles. And then he'd gotten turned around, something that had never happened to him before—or maybe the motel wasn't actually where the trucker thought.

But when he finally saw a porch light, the only thing he could do was run toward it before he collapsed against the heavy wooden door.

2

"What the fuck was that?"

Reed looked up from his computer screen to see Keith scowling at the door. "Probably just the wind."

"Wind doesn't sound like that."

"Animal?" Reed suggested, and Keith peered out the window because yeah, the last thing they needed was a deer running through the cabin looking for shelter from the storm.

"Don't see anything. Wait…shit." Keith still moved like a military man, because once a Marine, always a Marine. He opened the door swiftly and Reed came over in time to see a man's body crumpled on their porch.

The fierce storm blew snow and hail inside as Keith dragged the unconscious man inside. There was no telling what he looked like beyond Caucasian—his hair was covered with snow and he was bundled up, but it was no match for Mother Nature's wrath.

"Get those clothes off him—I'll get blankets," Reed barked, and Keith rolled his eyes like, duh, as he'd already

laid the boy down by the fire and had begun stripping the
wet clothing off the most likely hypothermic patient.

Reed raced to the bedroom for extra blankets and
towels, cranked the heat up in the house and grabbed his
medical bag. He'd started out as a medic in the Army and
had finished getting his medical degree while still in the
service. He'd been out for years now, in a private practice in
this small town when he'd settled in with Keith and Bobby.

Bobby.

The grief ripped through his chest, the pain still so fresh
it could bring him to his knees.

You couldn't save him, but you can save this one.

That got him moving forward. He tossed Keith the
blankets as they both knelt over the young man. Now that
Keith had brushed some snow off, he could see the light
brown color of the boy's hair. Lifted his lids to check his
pupils and was met with green eyes that didn't focus. He
was almost as tall as Reed, was in decent shape but much
thinner than someone with his frame should be.

He'd also recently been in a fight. There were bruises on
his knuckles and a large bruise on his side—Reed didn't
probe, as the man's skin would be too sensitive from the
hypothermia. Broken or badly bruised, his ribs would still
be a bitch to heal.

"Grab me the antibiotic and saline—wrap that in a warm
towel," Reed told Keith, who did so quickly, then returned
to searching the man's clothing while Reed started the

warm drip and the antibiotics after he readied an IV.

"Any ID?" he asked as he put the stick-on thermometer on the unconscious man's forehead and the stethoscope in his own ears and prepped to listen to his chest.

"No, but his name's Shane Wills and the address is a PO box, according to the junk mail he had stuffed in his pocket." Keith put the envelopes aside on a table so they wouldn't get lost. "He's got some cash, no credit. Nothing else in his pockets."

"Weird." Reed sucked his bottom lip as he continued checking Shane over. His temp was ninety-five, and he'd begun to shiver so hard Reed couldn't keep him still. "Hey Shane—you're safe. Can you open your eyes for me? Shane?"

At the sound of his name, the young man's eyes flickered open for a long second and then closed again. They'd been dulled with pain and fever, and Reed was worried.

"I'll check outside for a bag," Keith offered as the storm's intensity increased. "I'd hate to think he had family worried about him on Christmas Eve."

They'd planned to have a quiet dinner in so they'd had no worries about the storm. They'd weathered far worse.

Reed pulled the stethoscope out of his ears. "He's pretty sick on top of the hypothermia—we can't move him tonight in this weather safely. I've got enough antibiotics to get him through—tomorrow, we can see about checking him into the hospital. Forget going outside—take your clothes off."

Keith's brow shot up, and Reed just muttered something about him being a horny bastard.

Keith didn't argue, but he was already stripping down to his boxers. Probably knew that was the way things would go from the beginning—he was practically an honorary doctor after spending so much time with Reed.

Reed stripped too, stoked the fire and laid the comforter down while Keith crawled under the blankets and rolled Shane so Keith was pressed against his naked, shivering body, Shane's back to his chest. Reed quickly got under the blanket as well and pressed his chest to Shane's.

"He's freezing," Keith grumbled, but Reed noted he'd reached up to feel the boy's forehead like he could will his temperature back up. His dark eyes were intense, and for that moment, it was the first time Reed and Keith met, on the steps of this very house on a Christmas Eve what seemed like ages ago.

"You still look the same," Keith murmured, reading his mind as always. "Bullshit." And still, the man could make him blush.

They'd been together for eight years today, had been in love for most of that time, although for sure it had started with lust.

Nights like tonight reminded them that they were lucky to have one another. Made them miss Bobby too, although Reed suspected that would be an ache that neither man would ever be able to shake.

"You're thinking too hard," Keith told him now and Reed shrugged.

"Eight years ago, this was me," he reminded Keith, who he knew needed no reminding.

"Bobby and I never did this to you."

"Yeah, but you wanted to."

Keith smirked and didn't say anything else for a while.

Suddenly, Shane shifted hard against Reed. Murmured the name Kyle and pressed his lips to Reed's neck. And then he went still again.

Reed raised a brow at that, suddenly uncomfortably hard himself at the contact. "What happens when he wakes up?"

"He's either going to freak or he'll be in heaven," Keith said with a frown. "We can't let him come to like this."

"I don't think we've got a choice. I just want him to come to." Reed shifted and felt Shane's hand move down between their bodies. He looked down to see Shane circle his own cock, murmuring Kyle's name again as he stroked.

"Is he doing what I think he's doing?" Keith asked, and Reed breathed, "Yeah."

"Not a bad way for a man to warm himself up," Keith said, and the two of them waited, not wanting to do anything inappropriate with him but not wanting to stop him, either.

Under the heavy blanket, Reed began to sweat—he saw Keith had too and checked Shane's pulse with his free hand. Definitely not thready any longer. No, it was fast.

Shane began to breathe hard against his shoulder, his

body shifted, his hips rocking toward Reed's body as he stoked his broad cock. It was rock hard and hot, blood rushing to the organ and to other parts of the man's body as well.

There was no way to stop this. Reed saw the look in Keith's eyes—liquid desire, knew they'd both relive this in their fantasies for a long time to come.

When Shane came, it was with a sharp, keening cry. His eyes remained closed, his breathing sharpened and his skin was slick with sweat.

Mission accomplished.

Shane moved close to Reed, murmured "Kyle" and "missed you" a few more times and then fell back into the depths of the fever.

After half an hour, Reed checked Shane's temperature and stopped the warm saline so the guy's fever wouldn't spike up. Keith shifted out from under the blankets and grabbed a washcloth and fresh boxer briefs for Reed, who cleaned Shane's belly and chest, pausing to stare at his body.

"He's military," Keith declared, staring down at the younger man. "You think everyone's military."

"I knew you were."

"I was a doctor."

"Didn't matter." Keith watched Reed change out of the soiled black boxer briefs into the fresh pair. "I wonder if he's AWOL?"

"Are you going to check?"

Keith shrugged. "I'll see what I can pull up without triggering a manhunt. First, I'm going to look and see if he dropped a bag in the snow along the path."

He got up and pulled his clothes on, his cock achingly hard as he tucked it into his jeans. He glanced at Reed, who watched him and was so fucking grateful that someone looked at him like that after so much time spent together.

He pulled on a heavy jacket, and Reed told him, "Ten minutes," before Keith disappeared into the blizzard. He tracked down the path as best he could—Shane's footprints were long covered up, but he knew there was really only one way up the driveway through the massive trees that lined both sides of the drive. He'd lived here for ten years— bought the house with Bobby on a whim, which Bobby teased him about till his dying day.

"So impulsive," Bobby whispered to him the night before he died. "So unlike you."

It had been. He'd remembered being embarrassed to tell Bobby that he believed there was something magical about the place, because Marines didn't believe in magic—they believed in hard work. Country. God. Family.

But Bobby had believed in him and that had been all that mattered.

"Bobby, what are you doing?" he called into the howling wind and waited, like he expected a response.

"There's always a plan," Bobby had told him before his eyes had closed for good that night a year ago. Keith had never had a reason not to trust him.

3

Keith stomped the snow off his boots, stripped down and found that Reed had carried Shane into the spare bedroom, gotten him comfortable. There was a warm saline IV running into his arm and IV antibiotics on the bedside table.

"He's got pneumonia. I'll be monitoring him all night," Reed said.

"We'll be monitoring him all night," Keith corrected. "I didn't find any bag.

Let me go try to get the word out about him first."

He went into the small office on the other end of the living room and shot off some emails to friends who were still enlisted. He figured he should hear something back by the morning. He also checked local missing person's reports and found nothing. Something in his gut told him not to report Shane to the authorities, though.

The boy was in trouble—or he was trouble—Keith was sure of it.

Then again, he'd thought the same thing about Reed

when he'd shown up half dead on the doorstep on Christmas Eve, just the way the local legend said would happen. The realtor had been the one to tell Keith about it originally— she liked that bit of local flavor and thought Keith might as well.

Supposedly, the cabin was at least a hundred years old, and it had a reputation of bringing lovers together on Christmas Eve. People came there in bad weather, looking for an inn, but there was no record of an inn being on or near that property. There was a Motel 6 twenty miles away and nothing beyond that Keith had ever been able to find on any map, no matter how old.

No one had a clue where the inn rumor had started, but when Keith bought the house he'd inherited that story along with a good foundation, sixteen-foot ceilings and a nonexistent electrical system. Over the years, with Bobby's help and then Reed's, he'd rebuilt almost everything while keeping the original feel of the place.

And yeah, his sentimentality had definitely shown through.

From the outside, it looked like little more than a sturdy log cabin. It was exactly the way they liked it, because their business was as secret as their private life and it provided the men with the necessary security.

Having any kind of personal life or attachments as a mercenary was never recommended. Once anyone knew you had something—or someone—you'd rather die than lose, you were in trouble.

Keith and Reed had been off the grid for so long, it was a concern only at times like this. If Shane had been sent in to hunt them, he'd done a piss-poor job of it.

Keith would make sure it stayed that way and dammit, Christmas Eve and investigations didn't go together. He sipped his Scotch, the smell of ham and other foods cooking in the kitchen wafting over him. Reed had insisted on making a feast, and Keith's stomach rumbled appreciatively at the thought of the spread. Both men had learned to cook relatively well in their years in the military when they'd been living alone. Over the course of the years, they'd picked up a lot from Bobby too, who'd actually gone to culinary school at some point, just for fun.

Keith would've paid money to see that—an active-duty Marine in culinary school. Smiled thinking about Bobby using his KA-BAR knife to peel potatoes.

In a way, this meal was Reed's tribute to the man who'd died a week before Christmas last year. The men had promised Bobby they wouldn't stop celebrating theholiday.

Pulling his mind back to the present, Keith flexed his fingers over the keys, tapping into databases he had no business being in and coming up blank. That in and of itself brought up a number of red flags, in Keith's book.

"Anything?" Reed asked, coming into the den, leaning his hip against the desk facing Keith, who shook his head. "Special forces?"

"No way."

Reed seemed to agree. "Definitely military, which means this ID's fake.

Good, but fake."

"Shane's his real first name though—even half unconscious, he responds to it," Keith pointed out.

"Witness Protection?"

"I'll email Dan in case someone's missing. That's a Christmas Eve email no one would mind getting," he said, knowing the US Marshal would appreciate the heads-up.

"I'd hate to think of Kyle out looking for him. No one should be alone during the holidays," Reed said somberly as he moved closer to Keith.

They both had, at various points throughout their lives. "He's not alone."

"No, just shut in with one of the most suspicious men on the planet." Keith merely smiled because Reed said it with an affectionate rub to his shaved head, followed by a kiss. "I can still see the bite mark."

"You were a little excited," Keith said wryly, and Reed snorted. "Yeah, just a little. Not your fault at all."

"I was planning a repeat performance tonight, but I guess it'll have to wait."

"Looks that way."

Keith sighed. "When he wakes—"

"You are not going to interrogate him."

"You're really going to owe me," Keith told him

mutinously as Reed moved away and shrugged.

"Not a hardship," Reed called over his shoulder as he walked across the hall toward the guest room.

Through the open door, Keith watched his partner rub the young man down with water and alcohol. Managing fever on top of hypothermia took skill, but Reed had dealt with much worse.

After another hour of emails, including hearing back from Dan, his marshal contact, that all their WITSEC men and women were safe and sound, Keith got up and went to the doorway of the guest room, noting the flush of fever on Shane's face had subsided somewhat. But the boy's eyes still held that hazy, faraway look whenever they opened to Reed quietly saying, "Hey, Shane, can you open your eyes for me?" And then just as suddenly they'd close again and sleep would take him.

Reed looked up at him. "You okay?"

Keith put his hands up to grab the doorframe above his head, stretched himself as he gave an unconvincing, "Yeah."

"You've got to admit this is weird," Reed said finally. Of the three of them, he believed the least in that old legend about this house drawing those in need to it, but he couldn't deny the oddness of this. "I mean, eight years to the day. To the hour."

Keith shrugged. "'S'what the legend says. Travelers in need find their way here on this day at this time."

"Like me." Reed's blue eyes shone in the soft light, the

memories making him smile a little. His blond hair was on the longer side, and he was shorter than Keith—six-two to Keith's six-five, but his build was lankier. He was strong as hell, though, as Keith well remembered when he came to that night he woke on the living room floor and immediately tried to punch both Keith and Bobby.

Reed had war in his eyes. Sometimes, when he woke, he still did. He told Keith he always dreamed of the rain.

"There's no one like you," Keith told him. "We can't keep him here longer than tomorrow."

"There's your suspicious side coming through," Reed grumbled. "You know I'm right to be cautious."

"I know. He's beautiful, though," Reed murmured, and Keith rubbed a hand over his shaved skull as he moved forward toward the bed and wondered what the hell they were doing not calling the police.

"Yeah, a beautiful con artist," he muttered. Reed turned and shot him a sharp look as their patient suddenly opened his eyes and stared directly at Keith, a gaze that made him feel a sharp tug from gut to groin.

Fuck. It had been a mistake to let him in this far.

Shane struggled to sit up, but Reed was pressing his shoulders back down to the pillows. "Easy, big guy. You've been out of it for a while."

Keith held out the cup of water and Shane took a greedy pull from the straw, until he coughed. Reed eased him back, covered him back up and waited until he'd caught his breath.

"What's your name?" Keith asked.

Shane looked at him, a sudden confusion covering his handsome face. "It's um…fuck."

"Um fuck, huh?" Keith started, but Reed interrupted with a glare at Keith. "It's Shane Wills. Did you hit your head?"

"I don't remember," Shane admitted.

"What the hell were you doing out there?" Keith barked.

Shane pressed his lips together, shook his head as if attempting to clear it. "I don't know."

"What do you mean, you don't know? It's a simple question," Keith asked, but Reed put a hand against his chest to stop him, asked instead, "What's the last thing you remember, Shane?"

"I remember walking down a street in Philly…some guys hassled me and I fought them off, but not before I lost my wallet and they got in some good punches," he started slowly. "A truck driver took pity on me—cleaned me up and took me as far as here, I guess. When he dropped me, he told me there was an inn a mile from here. And then I walked."

Keith mentally cursed the driver for dropping this kid into the middle of nowhere in this weather. "No one's ever found that inn."

Because this *is the inn.*

He caught Reed's eye and both men fought a smile.

"And before that?" Keith pushed Shane, who shook his head.

"I don't remember. I've been trying to for the past few days—the whole ride…I was panicked."

"Maybe we should call the police—file a missing person's report—" Reed said.

"No!" Shane's hand shot out, grabbed Reed's wrist. "No."

Keith's eyes met Reed's. No doubt about it—Shane was nothing but trouble.

Not telling them much seemed like the best thing to do. Technically, Shane wished he couldn't remember shit, so maybe pretending not to remember wasn't such a big deal anyway. They seemed like all-right guys—former military, because he'd learned to spot them early on. But that would cause problems for him as well, because already, they didn't believe his story. Beyond that, they certainly didn't need his shit on their heads.

This was all a complication he didn't want and they didn't deserve. And him lying here, sick, weak, wasn't going to get him away from their prying eyes anytime soon. Not without major effort, and he was willing to give it that as soon as they gave him a little space.

He flicked a glance at each of them—both were good looking—Reed, the doctor, was blond and Keith's head was shaved, his eyes dark and his build broad. Reed was in shape too, although naturally slimmer. Keith had the bearing of a military man—he'd bet his life that the man was a Marine, but Reed also held the quiet edge to him.

Special forces, he thought to himself. *And you won't be here long enough to find out if you're right.*

"Shane, can you tell us a little more about...anything?" Reed asked.

What did they want to know about him? Much more than he was able to tell—and he knew the amnesia routine would wear thin quickly. To an extent, it already had in that Keith didn't seem to believe him and Reed was also somewhat skeptical.

Maybe telling total strangers would be easier. Maybe he could truly disappear from his old life and start over.

But every time he'd tried that, he was found. Followed. Tracked, like prey. Which was why staying in one place too long was never a good idea. "I already told you I don't remember anything else."

He closed his eyes again before they could say anything else to him. He heard them rustling around and then two sets of foot steps getting softer as the men left him alone. The door creaked a little, and when he looked from a slitted eye, he saw it was half shut.

Sleep, he told himself. *Sleep. Get stronger. And then get the hell out of here.*

But that old fight-or-flight feeling jangled through him

like a drug, and he knew it was now or never. Silently, he shifted out of the bed and pulled the IV out. Wrapped a piece of gauze to staunch the blood as he spotted his clothes by the chair. They were still damp, but they were better than nothing.

His training had kicked in—he could do things fast when necessary—it had been pounded into him to keep moving, whether or not he was half dead. Shane began to suspect the instructors liked the new recruits that way.

"Your comfort has never been, nor ever will be my concern" had been his drill sergeant's favorite line during Ranger school.

Silently, he moved out to the snow-covered deck and jumped into the soft, freezing snow. The hail hammered his face and he looked down before he continued.

He thought about how kind Reed had been and wavered for a second. Then he pictured Keith's scowl and continued along through the hip-deep snow and waded through to the trees he'd followed on the way up the driveway—it would lead him to the road about a mile down.

Better not to involve anyone else in his troubles. Kyle had already paid that price, and Shane didn't want any more blood on his hands.

He hadn't even realized the date until he'd heard Reed mention it. He shivered by the end of the first mile, hoped to hell a truck or a car was passing through with a Good Samaritan willing to pick up a total stranger on Christmas

Eve.

Reed checked on the food while Keith snagged some cold appetizers from thefridge.

"I'm starving," Keith told him.

"We'll eat soon—it's almost ready." Reed had lowered the stove and oven so nothing would burn. He took the ham out and left it covered while he popped in some other dishes and set the timer.

He glanced toward the half-closed door as the wind rattled the windows. "You think he's faking it?"

"You're the doctor. You and I both know that amnesia is really rare and usually has a medical explanation—like head injury or tumor."

Reed shook his head. "Could be emotional trauma."

"You're not buying it either. There's just something about this kid that makes you soft."

"Fuck you."

Keith laughed, because Reed couldn't tell him he was wrong. Instead, the big man moved to pull Reed closer. "He's not you."

"Could be," Reed mumbled, his face pressed against Keith's neck, liking the feeling of the solid body against his.

"Ah, Reed, come on."

But he knew he was breaking his lover down, the way Keith told him Reed always could. From the second he'd come into the man's life, Keith told him he couldn't resist him when he set his mind to something.

"Fine," Keith said. "We'll keep trying to help him. If he wants it."

The wind howled again and Keith's head jerked to the side as if he'd heard something else through the noise.

Both men went to the guest room to find it empty. Reed immediately went for his gear while Keith opened the door to the deck and tried to see out into the night.

When he came back in, Reed was already dressed for the weather, gun and flashlight at the ready.

"The kid's got a death wish," Keith grumbled, but Reed knew he was more pissed that Reed would be the one to go after him. Reed knew Keith's pissed-off attitude translated as worry for Reed, who appreciated that worry more than he could ever say. But while Keith had the brawn, Reed always had the tracking skills plus the necessary speed.

"You're just pissed he gave us the slip. Means we're getting old. And I'll be fine," Reed insisted.

Keith glowered at the getting-old remark. "If you're not back in twenty minutes—"

"I will be," Reed promised. In the cold was where he worked best, since his body always seemed to run hot, some kind of medical anomaly.

And although he never wanted to be near the desert again, hated the sand and heat and much preferred this weather, the snow that surrounded him could easily trigger his claustrophobia. To be fair, sometimes anything could, but now that he couldn't see his goddamned hand in front of his face, he had to stop, bend over and stare at his knees, because his boots were buried.

Ground yourself, dammit.

If he wasn't back in time, Keith would come looking for him. Knew he was already on shaky ground because of the holiday and Shane's arrival.

He drew a deep breath and then another, flashed back to the box with the vent and the wet on his lips, just like the wet from the snow. But this was freezing and that water hadn't been, and he was free to continue walking.

And finally, he did, pushed forward toward the side of the house and quickly followed Shane's path down the slanted land that led to the main road.

Reed had no problem catching up to him. Shane was weaving a little, although he had to give him credit for trying. Hell, he gave him credit for still being on his feet and having forward motion.

Definitely military.

He called Shane's name a few times so he didn't startle him, and Shane finally stopped, but he didn't turn. He accepted Reed's hand on his shoulder. And when Reed realized it wasn't going to work, he picked him up over his shoulder and double-timed it back to the house.

Keith was waiting, opened the door and took Shane from him.

"Hey, it was well under twenty minutes," Reed called as he stripped.

"Yeah, you made it by half a second," Keith told him as he put Shane down on the chair and got his clothing off so he wouldn't get the bed wet. By the time Reed got there, Keith had him tucked in and had the IV running.

"You warmed the blankets?" Reed asked. "Shut up, Reed," Keith warned.

"I know when to cut my losses," Reed told him, buried his face against Keith's chest as a form of thank-you, because he still had trouble saying the words after all these years.

4

Cold. So goddamned cold. He shivered, despite the fact he had long johns on under his uniform and tried to concentrate instead on the task at hand.

You're not back in Iraq with Kyle. You're feverish. In the Catskills somewhere.

But the dream pulled him in, and he could see Kyle's serious face as the older man placed a blanket over him and handed him a hot cup of bad coffee.

He was on the hard ground, unable to be moved. His ears were ringing. Kyle. Staring down at him.

"You're okay, brah. You're going to be just fine."

Shane couldn't actually hear the words, thanks to the roadside bomb exploding so close to him. But he read Kyle's lips and his eyes, because the man had always had such expressive eyes.

He put a hand up to Kyle's cheek. Wanted to express, yeah, I got you, but Kyle's eyes widened in surprise. It took Shane a few seconds to understand. Kyle's mouth opened, and Shane wanted to sit up, especially when he saw Kyle's face contort, a rictus of pain before his face went slack.

Shane tried to move, saw a figure move away, but not before he saw exactly who it was. But his attention pulled back to Kyle, who fell over to one side, on Shane's legs. Shane, who couldn't move himself. He screamed. At least he hoped he was, because he couldn't hear his own voice.

He was so goddamned cold.

Reed checked on Shane, who was restless as hell. His eyelids fluttered and he groaned, thrashed in sleep. Reed adjusted the meds. He didn't want to knock him out completely, because the fever was already doing a great job of that, but Shane was too agitated to let his body heal.

He hadn't worked fast enough though, because Shane let out the most heartfelt scream Reed ever heard. It was like a plea, like…

"He's mourning," Keith said from the doorway when the screams died down suddenly, cut by the narcotics Reed pushed.

Reed rubbed the goose bumps on his arms away, noted that Keith had come all the way into the room—the first time in days—and held Shane's hand.

"Think he's dreaming of Kyle?" Reed asked finally.

"He's seen combat," Keith said grimly. "Could be reliving that."

Reed wondered if he'd screamed like that. He must've, and more than once. "Don't go back there, Reed," Keith said quietly. A command. An order, despite the softness, and Keith was very good at giving them. Reed met his eyes—deep and dark. The keeper of all Reed's secrets—and God knew, there were a lot of them. "I swear to you, I will throw this kid out into the snow if this brings you back to that place."

Keith would never do that, but he would separate Reed from Shane. "I can do this."

"I know you can. But do you want to?"

Reed could drive Shane to the hospital. Could've done so two days ago when the storm broke and Keith went out to stock up on supplies before they were socked again. Their Christmas Ever dinner feast had lasted them for a good long time, even if they didn't get to start it until well into Christmas Day.

"I need to," was all Reed said. Keith continued to hold Shane's hand until the boy totally calmed. He knew they'd both noted the light band of scars that circled each wrist all the way around.

"They're about a year old," Reed noted.

"He's been held. Captured," Keith said quietly. Reed rubbed his own wrist unconsciously under the thick leather bracelet of Bobby's he always wore over it. His scars were older but otherwise the same. Deep. Ugly. Never going to heal.

Men like Reed never wanted to be held down. Sitting patiently wasn't in his DNA. Not in Shane's either.

Reed let Shane's wrist go after several long moments,

and Shane immediately tucked it under the pillow, like he was trying to hide it. Or like he was used to sleeping with a gun under his pillow.

"Look how he sleeps," Keith told Reed. Shane was on his stomach, one arm curled around the pillow, another stuck underneath his head and under the pillow and, if he'd had a weapon, Reed had no doubt Shane's hand would be wrapped around his gun right now. A classic pose for CIA, FBI, detectives…not really a military move, though.

"If he's been running from someone, that could explain it," Reed said as he stared at the boy with a little frown on his face. "He looks so young when he's sleeping."

"Because he is young." Keith turned to him. "At least you didn't use the word 'innocent.'"

"With a military man? Never." He reached for Shane's wrists, and the man restlessly moved but didn't wake as Reed exposed them. Keith stared at him for a long minute before Reed nodded. Keith took the two pairs of padded, binding cuffs and hooked one wrist and one ankle each to their closest bedpost.

"It's for his own good," Keith told him quietly.

"I know." But Reed's voice was quieter than he'd meant it to be.

Keith pulled the covers up over Shane's chest, put a hand on Reed's shoulder for a second and then walked out.

Reed followed after several minutes. Found Keith at the desk by the computer, a large sandwich on a plate next to him.

"Want half?" Keith asked as Reed reached for it.

"Forgot to eat," he mumbled around the food. Didn't say anything else until he'd finished that half and then the other, realized that Keith had actually made the sandwich for him. Because if Keith had handed it to him and told him he needed to eat, Reed would've refused. In many ways, he was more of a stubborn bastard than Keith.

He sank into the chair next to his partner, put his feet on the desk and sighed. His back ached—neck too—and he knew he needed a nice, long run along with some weightlifting. And sex. They were way overdue on something more than a quick shower and blowjob.

"Shane's ID isn't fake," Keith told him.

Reed's feet came down, and he was looking at the intel on the computer that Keith was definitely not supposed to have. But no one told a Force Recon Marine no.

Not often, anyway.

"Whoever erased him has to be high up. Is he being trained?"

Sometimes the CIA pulled promising candidates straight from the military for deep undercover work off the grid. Shane could be more dangerous than either man realized, although both had considered it. That was also why, especially now, Houdini was semi-shackled to the bed.

They needed to keep their own safety tantamount. Reed could always count on Keith for that—he was the one who made Reed feel protected during a time when no one else—not even Bobby—could.

"I'll dig a little more, but from what I can see, he was a good soldier. Being recommended for Ranger school, not Delta." Being recommended for Delta was rare, but it did happen. Reed was a living, breathing example. Part Creek on his mother's side, full Irish on his father's, he had both the bluster and the quiet. He was from a family of medicine and battle—it was in him from birth. When the time came to choose, he'd decided to combine both instead. He was a medic in Delta, and when he was on medical leave from the team, he'd decided to stay in the Army and go to med school, since he rarely slept anyway.

"Was there a Kyle in his company?"

"No." Keith sighed and pushed the keyboard away. "This is all Milsaps could give me."

"And you can't get anything else?"

"You're the one with the Army connections."

Reed grabbed his cell phone. iPhone. Whatever the hell it was. He never needed fancy—he just needed it to ring.

And it did. Prophet was on the other end. A good and dangerous man to know.

"Proph, it's Reed."

"Boy, you only call when you need a favor."

"Ditto, asshole. And who the hell are you calling boy?" Prophet hooted. "Hit me."

Reed gave him the intel, and Prophet promised he'd have

something within twenty-four hours. Reed heard bombs going off in the background and declined to ask where and what Proph was doing now.

"What're we going to do until then?" Keith asked as he stretched his big body in the chair. He looked like a growly bear, abs like steel and a grip to match. And Reed wanted all of that, wanted to motion for Keith to come hang with him on the couch. The fire was going, the storm had picked up, and their patient was resting comfortably.

But something was holding Reed back, and he had no clue what it was.

Bullshit. You know—you just don't want to deal with it.

"I've got to work out," Reed muttered, pushed out of the room, feeling Keith's eyes on him. And as much as he wanted the man to follow, he prayed harder that he stayed away.

Keith would give Reed the wide berth he needed—for now. But not for longer than the next twenty-four hours, because that's when the real trouble would begin.

He wasn't Bobby—Reed had never expected him to be. But Keith and Bobby were both kids of the streets, dumped into foster-care systems that beat them up and spit them out. They were both angry, chip-on-their-shoulder men who understood exactly what they needed.

Reed's desires were slightly more mercurial. When he'd come into their lives, they'd treated him with kid gloves. At first. It was only after Reed's first tantrum of sorts that they both realized that Reed needed the kind of handling Keith and Bobby could give him—and both men had been only too happy to show him so.

Now, Keith heard the click of weights moving up and down. Reed was spinning, grinding his gears, and Keith would stay up tonight and watch for any nightmares that might follow.

He could still hear Shane's screams in his ears. Only men who'd been through hell yelled like that, and only when their defenses were completely down. It was why most of the former military men Keith knew rarely slept, and when they did, they slept alone.

He hadn't slept alone for long stretches of time in years, and he was grateful for it. Heard the clink of the weights grow faster and pictured Reed's taut, sweaty body as he worked off some steam.

He had some other ideas about working things off, but he'd wait until the man came to bed. And while he had some time before that happened, he went into the steam shower, a place crowded with memories, all good, and he sat in the heat for a while and let himself reflect. At times like this, he always thought back to his first time withBobby.

He'd known the man since he'd enlisted at seventeen, but nothing happened until Keith turned twenty-one. Bobby was twelve years older, a celebrated Force Recon Marine who'd been called in to train new recruits and pick the best of the bunch. At the time, the special forces branches were all growing and they'd needed to handpick men rather than waiting for the men to come to them.

Keith had been one of the lucky ones chosen, hadn't known much about Force Recon before Bobby took him aside and explained what the elite force was all about. He'd stared at the broad man with nearly white-blond hair, buzz cut into a high and tight, and, if he looked back now, he'd admit that he'd fallen in love. At the time, he'd told himself he'd fallen in love with the idea of being a Force Recon Marine. For Bobby, Keith applied himself harder than he ever had in his life. He was built for all the punishment and camaraderie the Marines had to offer, reveled in it, grew the hell up, and fast. Learned to be a man instead of the street punk he'd been in very real danger of becoming.

It took a year before he was through the basics of Force Recon training, but he'd passed the most important tests. He'd also managed to drive Bobby fucking nuts, and he hadn't really been sure why at the time.

Okay, yeah, he'd been kind of sure, because he'd wanted to be with the man for years. Bobby had an open-door policy, widely rumored, that had men showing up to his door at midnight on Saturdays. If the porch light was on, it was first come, first served.

No one would ever admit to being there, but Keith had a feeling more than a few guys he'd known had. He'd never gotten up the balls to do so, probably because he was afraid

Bobby would tell him he was too big a pain in the ass and turn him away.

But he wasn't thinking about any of that the night he'd learned he'd be continuing on with the training. That night had been for celebrating. Letting his guard down, for the first time in what felt like forever. He recalled dancing. On tables. Cheering. A lot of bluster from a lot of Marines. And then he was dragged out of the back of the club by Bobby. Stood face to face with the man who outranked him and whose service he would be under for the next who knew how many years, and remembered how much he'd mouthed off to him lately.

He could, unfortunately, do nothing but laugh at that moment, barely remember his own name. And he'd been far too drunk to adequately defend himself, especially since Bobby bound and gagged him efficiently and threw him in the back of his SUV. When they got to Bobby's house, he dragged Keith inside and bound his arms behind him and to a chair, with rope around his chest as well. The bonds were so tight he couldn't move his upper body, and he didn't dare move his legs, or he knew they'd be tied before he could protest. He'd take his freedom in small doses.

And then, Bobby took the gag out of his mouth. Keith coughed. Bobby gave him water and Keith drank it down, wondering if this was all part of some bizarre Force Recon initiation. Because, according to the notice he'd received, he'd passed muster, been accepted.

When he looked into Bobby's eyes, he knew this was about so much more than a new position.

"What are you going to do to me?" he couldn't help but ask. If he'd been sober, he would've kept his mouth shut. He'd gotten in trouble with Bobby before during training— and although Bobby always kicked the shit out of him, he'd never done anything like this.

"I'm going to do something to make you finally understand who is in charge here." Bobby leaned in close to Keith's face, his drawl heavy and smooth. "And by the time I'm done you're going to be my obedient little Marine who does anything I ask."

Keith shivered involuntarily as Bobby ran a finger along the front of his neck, using it to push up under Keith's chin to keep the eye contact. "That's what I want to see. I like to see you a little afraid of me. Not sure what I'm going to do with you, not sure what's going to happen here tonight, knowing there's no way to get out of it…all this is going through your mind right now. You can't escape, can't move, and even if you could, you'd be disobeying another direct order from your commanding officer." Bobby paused for a minute and then, without warning, ripped Keith's shirt open. Buttons went flying as Bobby pulled it off his shoulders as far as it could go.

Keith drew some rapid breaths and felt the faint sense of dread as Bobby smiled at him for the first time since this began.

"Now, tell me you're going to follow my next orders, even though you really don't have a choice. Say, 'I'll do anything you ask me to, Bobby'. No questions asked. Say it."

Keith cleared his throat, but when he spoke, his voice was still hoarse. "I'll do anything you want, Bobby." He squirmed slightly in the seat under the man's intense gaze. "No questions asked."

"Good boy. Do you want to know what's going to happen? What I want you to do next?" He asked as he moved his hands to Keith's waist. Keith nodded, not trusting his voice anymore. "I'm going to take these off." He gave Keith's jeans a tug, pulling them down below his hips.

Keith drew in another sharp breath and bit his bottom lip as Bobby continued, "And you're going to ask me to put you inside my mouth and make you come. And then I'm going to put you into my mouth. And you're going to come for me, come right inside my mouth like a good little Marine. And while I'm working on you, I want to hear you tell me how you feel, let me know you like what's happening to you. I want to hear you call out my name. What do you think about that?" Bobby finished and sank to his knees between Keith's legs.

The whole world went still then, even as Keith's mind continued to spin. "I'm waiting," Bobby finally remindedhim.

Keith licked his lips, his mouth dry, and looked away from Bobby.

"No, Keith. I want you to look into my eyes when you ask me. Right into my eyes, so I know you mean it. And I want you to keep watching me the whole time, especially when you come."

Keith didn't answer with words. Instead, he whimpered softly, trying to catch it before Bobby heard it.

It only served to make Bobby smile wickedly.

Keith closed his eyes for a minute, as though when he opened them this would be another one of his dreams. Another one of his extremely erotic dreams that he'd been having over the past year, all starring Bobby. They'd wake him up in the middle of the night, and he'd be sweating, breathing hard and blushing. But this was the point where his dreams always ended, right before Bobby was about to take him.

Now Keith opened his eyes, slightly disoriented from all the drinking he'd done, and he looked down.

Bobby was positioned right between his legs, which were spread wide, thanks to the restraints. Keith's pants were off and he was obviously aroused. And Bobby was waiting patiently for him to speak.

It wasn't a dream at all.

Keith knew he had no choice, and finally spoke the words Bobby had given him to say.

"Put me inside your mouth, Bobby. Make me come." His voice was rough with want now, even though he was still nervous.

Wordlessly, Bobby put his head down and took as much of Keith as he could into his mouth. Keith uttered a long, low moan of acquiescence and watched the man's head move up and down as he felt himself being dragged over Bobby's teeth and tongue. He didn't even have to try to follow the man's orders, because within minutes the words just flowed out of his mouth, mixed with uncontrollable moans that ripped from his throat.

"Oh God, feels so fucking good, Bobby. Please don't stop…yeah, that's it. Just like that. Please, keep your tongue there." The only thing Keith could move were his hips, and he was arching them toward Bobby, who put his hands firmly on Keith's hips, grounding them.

That made Bobby wilder. And then he went in for the kill, deep-throating Keith's cock in and sucking, forcing him to a climax.

"Fuck, Bobby—I'm going to come. Bobby, please…I love you," he heard himself cry out as he came in a shuddering rush in Bobby's throat.

He was no longer looking at Bobby the way he'd been ordered to. But obviously that minor transgression was okayed because Bobby didn't say anything. Not until he finally worked up the courage to open his eyes, praying this wasn't all some big joke.

"So that's what it took to get you to admit your feelings." Bobby stood and kissed Keith, letting Keith taste himself. He heard the moans drumming up in the back of his throat again, especially when Bobby began handling his cock.

When he drew back, he said, "Don't forget, I'm still in charge here. And I'm not through with you yet. Not by a long shot."

He released Keith's legs and arms. "You're going to follow me upstairs and lay yourself out on my bed. And I'm going to fuck you—and you're going to keep telling me in that sweet way of yours just how you feel about me. And you're going to look right in my eyes as you do. Do you understand?"

"Sweet?" he heard himself say, and Bobby laughed then.

"Still haven't quite mastered the whole obedience thing, have you, honey?"

"I guess not." He sat there, thoroughly debauched and Bobby waited, probably more patiently than the man ever had. "Look...I...shit."

"Can you just follow my goddamned orders?"

Okay, yes, Keith could do that, because it was much easier than saying what he needed to. He marched up the stairs and into Bobby's room and laid himself out on his bed. The big man came in and straddled him, half naked himself at this point.

"You're scared," Bobby said and Keith nodded. "You've never done this before."

Keith flushed, went to try to push Bobby off him but he was stopped. "Did I say that was a problem? I like that you're a virgin. I knew you were."

To his goddamned horror, he felt tears form in his eyes. "Stop. Breathe. Say what you need to."

"I can't fucking do this until I know how you feel about me. Because I've never had this. Never felt this way about anyone—"

"I know how you grew up, Keith. And as for how I feel about you, couldn't tell all these months, couldn't tell by the way I looked at you? No, of course you couldn't. You were too busy getting in trouble, looking for my undivided attention." Bobby was teasing him, his tone gentler than Keith had ever heard it as he realized Bobby was right on the money.

"You still haven't answered my question," Keith said, surprising both of them with his boldness. "Because I can't do this without knowing if you don't feel the same, I can't let you break my heart."

"Just when I think I know you, you go and blow me away," Bobby had murmured, had looked right into Keith's eyes. "I think I've loved you from the second I met you."

Keith realized there were tears shining in his eyes as he came back to the present. That damned Marine could always surprise him, right up until the end. He and Keith fought side by side for several years before Bobby retired, with Bobby doing private work until Keith had put in his time.

They'd worked side by side, enjoying the adrenaline rush and not having to worry about the prying eyes of the military.

Fourteen years.

You had some chip on your shoulder, Marine, he heard Bobby whisper in his ear.

And Reed had an even bigger one.

For the first time in days, Keith felt confident that he could handle it.

Shane woke to groans. Sex sounds, but he'd been dreaming about Kyle for the entire time he'd been out as if it had been one continuous loop of alternating pleasure and pain. Maybe he'd been groaning.

Shit.

It took him a while to realize he'd been drugged and also shackled to the bed. Fear raced through him, because even though he knew where he was, he'd never be rid of that instinct. He yanked on the cuffs, yelled, bucked against the bed, until Reed and Keith came in and stood on either side of him.

"Stand down, boy, before you hurt yourself," Keith said, his voice sharp. "We're keeping you safe."

Shane believed him and stopped struggling. He felt the handcuffs releasing. "Come on, sit up," Reed urged. "You'll be shaky. I gave you meds for the fever and your anxiety."

Shane couldn't move fast this time even if he wanted to. His head felt fuzzy, stuffed with cotton, swollen with memories. But the cold soda Reed offered felt good going down. Sugar helped everything. So did the painkillers that made him forget his aching ribs.

"You look better," Keith told him. "Climbing out of here in a storm was a stupid move."

He knew that. "Look, I'll get out of your way. I'll find the inn the trucker mentioned."

"Don't bother," Keith said. "Do you have family we can call?"

He knew most of his military records were sealed, but his family backstory could be—would be—found by these men eventually, so he offered, "My dad died last year. My mom's got Alzheimer's—I sold the house to pay for the facility she's in. Doesn't remember who I am."

"I'm sorry, Shane," Reed said and then asked, "Who's Kyle? Should we call him?"

Who's Kyle? A simple question. A loaded question.

Kyle's the man who died because of me. Kyle was the man I loved.

"Kyle was my brother." Technically not a lie, because of the whole brothers- in-arms thing. And even though he knew these men slept together didn't mean they would necessarily be accepting of him in that respect.

"Bullshit."

He stared up at Keith. "What are you talking about?"

"You jacked off in your sleep, came calling Kyle's name," Reed said, his voice gentler than Keith's.

He opened his mouth but no sound came out. His cheeks heated, and he struggled to remember doing that, but couldn't.

"It's all right that you were lovers. We're okay with that," Reed told him and it clicked into place. The sex sounds. He hadn't been making them in his sleep— those sounds had been coming from Keith and Reed's room.

"It's all right because you guys are gay?"

"Yes," Keith said like Shane was the stupidest human being on the planet. "Okay, yeah, Kyle and I were together for two years. He died, and I'm just out of sorts. With everything."

There was no reason they shouldn't believe that. Grief fucked everybody up, and this time, Shane had told the complete and utter truth.

"So you're just bumming rides around the country, trying to find yourself?" Keith asked.

"It sounds stupid when you say it, but yeah." The big man would continue to challenge him at every turn, it seemed.

"Keith, cut him a break."

"He's hiding something." Keith wasn't letting him off the hook, and Shane found himself squirming under the man's scrutinizing gaze. "Your amnesia story was crap. Why wouldn't this one be?"

"Kyle died and I loved him." He stopped short of saying anything more because his voice started to break. Finally he added, "Why bother? You're never going to trust me."

"Might, if I start getting more of that truth you just gave me," Keith said. "Why's it so important to you that I trust you anyway?"

"It's not." Lie. But this time, Shane had no idea why.

Keith just snorted and left the room. Reed stayed, and after some more gentle quizzing, with Shane obstinately insisting there was no one for them to call, no family or friends who'd be worried or missing him, Reed left him alone. The fever began to spike again, not as high as before, but enough to drain him.

"How long have I been out?" he asked, his lungs starting to feel tight again. He coughed after he said it, and Reed gave him a pillow to hold against his ribs while he did so. And then Reed rubbed his back and gave him more medicine. And a breathing treatment.

I'm a fucking invalid.

"You were out for four days," he told Shane when he could breathe a little easier again.

"I don't want those restraints again," Shane said quietly before the blond man left him alone.

"You can't leave. You'll die out there."

"I know that. I'll stay," he promised, and he meant it. Mainly because he didn't have the strength or the will to fight it anymore, no matter how dangerous it all was.

Reed nodded, took the cuffs with him when he left the room.

After he stepped out, something compelled Reed to go back in and try a few more questions. Now that Shane was feverish again, but not so much so that he was incoherent, it seemed like some answers he needed might slide out Shane's mouth without much coercion.

Not fair, of course, but tricks of the trade never were.

He put the cuffs on the couch and went back to Shane's bedside. Shane didn't seem surprised at all, less so when Reed spoke.

"You were in the Army." A statement, not a question, and Shane nodded, caught off guard a little. So much for amnesia. Reed had known Keith was right, but at least the big man wasn't here to smirk about it.

"For six years, yes." He was too out of it to ask how Reed knew, and Reed didn't see it pertinent to offer that information.

"How long have you been out?" Reed continued.

"Four months. Maybe five. I've lost track." Shane paused and then shot back, "How long have you and Keith been together?"

Ah, so maybe not so out of it after all. "Eight years."

"He's a Marine."

"I guess it's easy enough to tell. Yes. And I was Army. You're in good hands here."

Shane's face fell a little bit. "I don't deserve all of this. I've caused you a lot of problems."

"You've caused yourself a lot of problems. Keith and I are fine. I know you'll tell me everything when you're ready."

"How can you be so sure of me when Keith's not?" Shane asked.

"Shane, do you need a safe place to stay?" Reed demanded, keeping his voicedown.

Shane looked him in the eyes. "Yeah, I do."

"Then you'll stay here and we'll fucking figure it out, soldier. All right? But for now, I need you to rest so you don't relapse. You don't realize how sick you were. And you still are."

Shane's face flushed from the speech, but partially from the fever. He managed to say, "Okay", and Reed could tell he was holding back tears.

"I know what it's like to mourn someone. Trust me. Keith and I both do."

"I do trust you. I don't know why, but I do," Shane told him.

"Good. Then lie back and go to sleep. I'll make you some dinner for when you wake. By then, you'll be hungry."

He listened, tucked himself in and closed his eyes the second his head hit the pillow. Reed left the door open and reached into his pocket for his phone, which had been buzzing for the last ten minutes.

Proph had given up on calling and had just emailed him—short and sweet, and Reed glanced in at the sleeping

Shane before heading toward the bedroom where Keith waited.

"You get anything else out of him?"

"He admitted he was in the Army. And I heard from Proph. He was dishonorably discharged."

"But he didn't tell you that part himself."

"No," Reed admitted. "But it just doesn't sound like him."

"Because you know him so well."

Keith had his arms folded across his chest. He was pushing Reed's buttons, purposely, and Reed might've known why, but that didn't mean he had to like it. And he sure as hell didn't.

"I'm not allowed to have intuition? Because it's kept me alive for a damned long time."

"Ditto," Keith said, and Reed couldn't argue with that. Didn't want to argue at all. Only time would tell whose intuition would pan out.

Night blended into day. Shane's sleep was long and fevered and interrupted often by meds and fever-breaking sweats and dreams. He wasn't sure it was illness alone. He figured he was partially in mourning, which he'd avoided for as long as possible. This was the culmination of months and months on the run, attempting to hold it together.

He'd finally failed. Thankfully, he wasn't alone as he paid the price.

The worst was waking up to his own screams. At first, he'd barely skim the surface, unable to stop the panic himself, not until he felt Reed's or Keith's touch. They talked to him in low, comforting voices. Reassured him. He knew they stayed in bed next to him sometimes and he was too grateful to be ashamed he needed that.

At times, they'd soak him in cool cloths, wiping his forehead and cheeks and chest. Once, he remembered fighting them when they lowered him into a cold bath. But then the fever broke and he calmed. He slept against Keith's chest, woke in the morning, alone and wondering if it had all been adream.

But it hadn't been. Because as he got his strength back, they brought him food. Put movies on. Sat with him until he fell asleep, usually making it no more than twenty minutes in.

He'd catch snippets on their conversations. It was apparent how close they were, half the time finishing each other's sentences. He heard the name Bobby sometimes and their tones would grow somber. Other times there would be laughter and teasing.

It was weeks past the New Year when he was well enough to declare himself fine.

"You're better, but you're nowhere near fine," Reed corrected him immediately. "You need rest now more than ever, because you'll be a prime candidate for relapse."

He wanted to complain but he was alive. The men understood his restlessness, brought him books and magazines and a laptop to help. Keith walked with him across the porch that extended along three quarters of the cabin, making him wrap himself like a mummy to do so.

Reed said the cold air was good for his lungs.

He was weak, but being in good shape before all of this started helped him a great deal.

Plus, he was hardheaded, as Keith told him more times than he could count.

Keith was at least six foot five. He was big by nature but not like some beefed-up muscle guy. He worked out but he moved gracefully for someone his size. Reed was tall and lean, moved near silently and always seemed to catch Shane when he was about to do something he wasn't supposed to, like get out of bed himself.

He was getting more irritable as the days passed. Horny too. "Means you're almost back to normal," Reed told him.

"Just leave me the hell alone," he muttered. And that night, when he found himself exactly that, he regretted telling them to stay away. Jerked himself off twice with no real relief. Slept. Woke screaming after he had the dream about the day he'd heard Kyle screaming and stared at his wrists like he'd expected them to be still chained.

Fuck. He never had that part of the dream—never let himself go there. He blamed the illness and the drugs.

He was bathed in sweat. Shaking. Sure the fever had returned but the thermometer confirmed no. Reed brought in the basin and washcloths anyway. As Shane sat in the middle of the bed, unable to share because he was engulfed in his silent pain, Reed washed him down. Patted him dry. Made him drink sugary soda and take pain meds.

He didn't allow himself to cry until Reed left. Reed came back in several minutes after he'd stopped sobbing, further cementing Shane's belief that the man knew just about everything, including when Shane needed him.

"He's finally asleep," Reed said as he finally dragged into bed sometime after three in the morning after a couple more weeks of monitoring Shane and his illness. He was getting better but it was a slow, uphill battle and the freezing early February temperatures weren't making things easier.

"He's a cranky bastard," Keith muttered as he put down the iPad in favor of giving Reed's shoulders a much-needed massage. Reed moaned gratefully, moved his head from side to side, cracking his neck in the process.

"He's better, and right now, that's all that counts," Reed declared, hearing the exhaustion heavy in his voice—he'd slipped back into the heavy drawl that always came out more during those times. "We played poker. He took all my cash."

Keith snorted. "He's definitely better. Told me to fuck off last night."

"No shit?"

"With his back turned, muttered under his breath when he thought I'd left the room."

"And he's smart too." Reed knew Shane had started to grow on Keith. When he found Keith in bed with Shane after one particularly long, worrisome night, he knew letting Shane go might not be the best option.

And after his initial tries at escape, Shane didn't seem to have a problem with staying, no matter how restless he'd gotten.

"He was really sick, wasn't he?" Keith asked, although

he knew, had watched Reed fighting the fever as the storm barreled in and snowbound them. If need be, they could've gotten him to a hospital, but there wouldn't be much more that could be done for him. It was meds, keep the fever down and faith that everything would turn out the way it was supposed to.

It had taken those first forty-eight hours after Shane tried to escape before he finally turned the corner from needing the intensive care unit to merely being very sick. In the meantime, Reed consulted with another doctor down the road who concurred with the course of treatment. Pneumonia took time to break, and finally, Reed had heard the clearing in Shane's lungs, felt the coolness of his forehead.

After that, it was a matter of keeping him from doing too much while not letting him remain bedridden. They walked him around, used the coughing machine to get the junk out of his lungs.

He got stronger day by day.

"Yeah, he was sick. But I don't think that's all of it. I think...maybe he's mourning Kyle. I don't know how long ago he died—didn't want to pry or piss him off—but it's like, I don't think he'd ever let himself mourn before this." He collapsed back on the bed when Keith finished the massage, stared at the ceiling. "He's been running from it."

"Can't blame him."

"I don't think he's got anywhere else to go."

"I wasn't planning on kicking him out into the snow tonight."

He turned on his side to stare at Keith as the man flipped through pages of guns and ammo on his iPad. "Well, you're just so damned generous, aren't you?"

"You know it." Keith favorited some pages with quick flicks of his finger. Reed had always loved the man's fingers—they were thick and strong, with perfect, clean blunt-cut nails. Now, he reached out to thread his fingers through Keith's free hand, pulled it to his mouth and kissed the top of it. "Now you're just sucking up."

"That's not sucking. I can show you sucking."

"Less talking, Army boy."

Reed snorted but allowed Keith to pull him close. "You're leaving in a few days."

"You gonna be all right here with him?" Keith asked in all seriousness. "Yeah, I will be. But if you're going to stress about this while you're away—"

"I won't. If I thought I would, I'd never have taken the job. Shane's sick—he needs to get better. Once that happens…"

"Once that happens, it'll happen," Reed said. "Now shut up and fuck me, all right?"

Keith sensed it first, but Reed was by his side in seconds. Both men had hastily dressed and shoved on boots, and they ignored the weather. Reed had his weapon and he said, "Cover me," as he slid around the side of the house. Keith remained in place, not able to leave Shane inside unprotected.

He hoped Shane remained inside, didn't wake and come looking for them.

He took the binoculars and scanned the outer perimeters for snipers.

"Second set of prints. Boots, size nine, headed to and from the woods," Reed confirmed. "House intact—he didn't plant anything."

Which meant no bombs or bugs.

"Is this blowback from a job?" Keith wondered out loud.

"Don't know. But I'll gear up and take the ATV into the woods."

"I'm going with you."

"You can't. Shane can't stay alone."

As if he needed reminding. "He can handle himself— and weapons."

"I don't want him to wake up screaming again," Reed reasoned. "Let him think he's still safe. Don't ruin it."

Keith wanted to tell Reed that it wasn't fair, that he deserved to know. But he understood Reed wanting to give Shane any kind of peace he could. And when Reed came back out quickly, more fully armed, and jumped on the ATV, Keith wondered if he'd ever thought about the fact that whoever was out there might not be for them, but rather, coming for Shane.

The bigger question was why.

He checked the area through the binoculars again. Got a few texts from Reed that the tracks went down to the road, where they met with tire tracks from an SUV.

He would follow them as far down the road as he could, see what direction they went.

Which might tell them nothing. There were very few places to stay around here, unless he was staying with friends.

Could be a hunter, Keith told himself. Could all be a false alarm. But it never was.

Reed followed the tracks to the main road—there was no point in attempting to go farther, since it was a muddy mess of tire tracks mixed with ATV and footsteps. What was important was that he'd been right—there had been eyes on him.

He promised himself that he'd never ignore his gut feelings again as he roared up the road back to the cabin. The next storm was rolling in—the past month had brought the messiest weather Reed remembered seeing since…

Since Christmas Eve and that entire winter, eight years ago.

Keith was still waiting for him on the porch. He pulled up next to the man and cut the engine.

"Whoever it is, he's been watching us for weeks," Reed said, and Keith unconsciously turned his head halfway toward the cabin's doorway. They were both thinking the same thing.

"You said you thought he was running from something. Looks like it's someone," Keith said now.

"He's not ready to tell us."

"That shouldn't matter," Keith said.

"But we both know it does. He's in trouble. He's scared. And that's what we do—we protect people."

"People who ask for our protection," Keith argued.

"I'd say waking up screaming means he needs some kind of protection," Reed retorted. "We should just put up extra security measures here."

"And we don't tell Shane any of it?" Keith asked. "Because maybe he knows what's going on. Maybe he's bringing danger to our door."

"I'm not saying you're wrong. But…don't ask him yet, Keith. Please. For me."

"Dammit, Reed." Keith's voice was angry, but his eyes held the understanding Reed needed tosee.

Someone was stroking his cheek. He wanted to murmur "Kyle", but he knew that wasn't right. The touch was different. Even in his sleep he was actively pressing his cheek to the hand, nuzzling it.

The scent was familiar. He liked it. He might've even groaned a little in his sleep.

And then the whole being-watched feeling overtook the pleasure, and he grasped the wrist of whoever it was. Hard.

It was pulled away equally so. He heard footsteps, and he rolled out of bed, standing before he was anything close to fully awake and remembering things. Like Keith and Reed, their cabin. And the fact that his ribs ached like a mother because he'd been pushing too hard.

He blinked, grabbed the side of the bed and saw Keith watching him. "What the hell?"

"I didn't expect you to jump out of bed like that. I was just checking on you." Keith's voice was gruff from getting caught even as Shane leaned back against the mattress. As much as he wanted to crawl back in, he knew that would hurt and he was still trying to catch his breath from the overriding, intense pain that first movement caused.

He could still feel Keith's fingers that had been stroking his cheek. "You're overdoing it with the ribs."

"Tell me something I don't know."

"You need a shave," Keith continued, making no move to help Shane. "Unless you're going for the mountain-man look."

It was a good excuse for Shane to touch his face where Keith's fingers had been. His beard was rough but not weeks old. One of them had shaved him a few days ago, and his dick got hard just thinking of him lying there while Keith shaved him.

Fuck. He didn't know he had that kind of a kink.

He turned toward the bed to hide his sudden erection and winced again as the pain got sharper. He grabbed the blanket, twisted and tried to sit, and heard himself groan.

Keith was next to him, cursing, helping him into bed. Keith took most of his weight on so it wasn't as bad as it could've been, but he was out of breath from the pain. He curled on his side, unmoving, waiting for it to subside so he could do the important things, like breathe.

"You did that to yourself," Keith told him as his hands splayed along Shane's bare side. He'd barely worn clothes since he'd gotten here. Like a fucking nudist colony, this place was, although, granted, he had none of his own clothes here anyway. Reed told him they'd basically had to cut the frozen clothes off his body that first night.

He'd had shorts on at some point, but he got hot and restless when he slept lately and ended up naked most times when he woke. "Leave me alone."

"Not while you're sleeping in my guestroom," Keith snapped. But nothing in the harshness of his words matched the gentle touch of his hands along Shane's side. Shane held his breath, thinking it would hurt, but the probing didn't do anything but make him hard. Again.

Dammit.

"Take these," Keith told him. Held out two pills that would probably knock him on his ass again, and Shane considered refusing. But although he could be stoic, he was far from stupid. He accepted them, slugged them down with a cold Coke Keith handed him, the sugary goodness giving him a rush.

"Got any chocolate?" he asked, and Keith handed him a box of Hostess cupcakes. He glanced between the box, and Keith and wondered how the man knew, why he was so prepared. "Did I ask for these before?"

Keith didn't answer that, instead asked, "What the hell happened to you?" probably for the thousandth time. Shane had lost count. And he told the same story every time, knowing Keith was listening for inconsistencies.

"Told you, I got rolled." Fuckers jumped him when he was down, and although he managed to knock two of them out, a third had gotten away with his bag. He'd found it abandoned a few blocks away, because it only contained clothes and he didn't feel like picking his crap out of the garbage.

He'd been in a truck traveling northeast ten minutes later. And he didn't want to think about any of that, what he left behind, what might be coming for him. In the eye of the storm, he was protected and cracked ribs or not, suspicious Marine on his six, he was safe for the moment.

Keith watched Shane eat two cupcakes in a row and unwrap a third. They were Reed's favorite and they appeared to be Shane's as well, although to be fair, he seemed like an equal opportunity sugar whore.

But the chocolate couldn't heal Shane, and he was still breathing shallowly, which was the reason the pneumonia hit him so hard. Now, he touched Shane's side again, lightly, pretending not to notice Shane jump at the touch, pretending not to see the shiver go through his body and the goose bump trail, even though Keith's hands were warm.

Interesting, and Keith cursed himself for being interested at all. He forced himself to focus on the injury instead. The bruising was yellow now, making the contusions looking uglier as they spread along his ribcage and lower back.

"It's healing nicely, don't you think?" Shane asked sarcastically with a mouthful of cupcake.

"I think they were broken."

"Not," Shane offered as helpfully as possible through the chocolate. Keith wanted to smile but bit it back. Because this kid was goddamned fucking charming him by just being himself, despite the fact that he was still closed off about his past and pretending he just happened to show up on their doorstep by sheer luck.

Well, that last part might be the truth, but everyone who came here was running from something. That's just the way it was.

"You're enjoying those cupcakes—I would've brought more, had I known."

"Next time, two boxes would work. Milk woulda been good with these, but this will do," Shane mumbled as he washed down another cupcake with the rest of the soda. All that caffeine would fight with the narcotics Keith had given him, but the pain pills were strong enough to win. Keith took the wrappers and can as Shane got himself comfortable and wondered when he'd voluntarily turned into a nursemaid for a man who wouldn't answer the simplest of questions.

At least he'd dropped the amnesia routine.

Shane murmured, "Thanks," and touched his hand to his cheek for a moment, rubbing the way Keith had been. He couldn't help it—Shane looked so damned peaceful and handsome.

"Welcome," Keith said, hearing the gruffness in his voice

again.

Shane pulled the pillow over his face now, burrowing under it so he could escape the light. Keith recognized it as habit. He wanted to ask Shane another question but he could see by the deep, easy breaths that he was already asleep.

That was definitely a military habit.

"Is he all right?" Reed asked and Keith forced himself not to jump guiltily, but he was caught just the same.

"Fine." He turned and brushed past Reed with the garbage in his hands. "He's eating chocolate at an alarming rate. He's more of a sugar addict than you are."

Reed frowned at the box of cupcakes, since there was only one left. He snagged it, unwrapped it and stuffed half of it in his mouth like Shane was going to jump up and eat it out from under him at any moment. "I'm going to have to start hiding my stash," he muttered around a mouthful of frosting. "'Cause these are my favorites."

"Of course they are."

"Thanks for checking on him."

"Yeah, yeah. Can't have him dying in our guest room," Keith groused. "You are a regular Santa Claus."

"I'll show you my bag of toys if you keep that up," Keith warned and Reed had the good sense to at least blush a little.

"Maybe we can incorporate chocolate into that somehow?" Reed asked hopefully, and Keith reached out with his free hand and pulled him close. Kissed him and said, "I can work with that."

Reed tugged him away from the guestroom and toward theirs. "Come on— let me give you a proper send-off."

7

Keith left the next morning at O-dark-hundred, during a lull between storms. He'd been taken by helo off the property as Reed watched the bird rise above the snow-capped trees and take off like a shot. He'd stayed on the porch until he couldn't hear the bird's roar any longer and he'd gone inside and made breakfast.

Keith would be gone anywhere from forty-eight hours to a week. With Shane here, he wouldn't be alone, and he couldn't say he wasn't grateful for that. The past year, the cabin felt so damned lonely when Keith went on trips, and while Reed wasn't afraid of being by himself by any means, having company would help as he tracked Keith through his mission. Otherwise, he would sit and stew over computer readouts and bother Prophet too much.

Granted, he'd still do that, but having Shane here would keep his mind slightly less occupied on every aspect of the mission that could go wrong. As he settled into the couch to relax for a few hours before he had to begin tracking Keith, he looked around the quiet comforts of the cabin and thought about how much he loved this dammed place. There wasn't much to it, to the naked eye, but inside they had every comfort creature imaginable.

There were long winters up here. They were prepared for any eventuality by now, having perfected it over the past years. They had plenty of food, natural gas automatic generator plus a back-up, wood they'd stockpiled and medical supplies. Jobs were shelved—and if they were really important, Prophet sent a chopper in for them, as he just had. It landed on the field they'd stripped clear for that purpose.

But they hadn't been prepared for Shane, and the tensions were building, mainly for Reed. He tried to keep himself calm but he couldn't get himself there. And Keith wasn't pushing him all that hard because of their guest and the confines of the cabin. The second floor held all their crap necessary for jobs, but it wasn't ready for humans or sex. And their young, beautiful, half-naked houseguest who thought nothing of walking around in shorts while his fever broke wasn't helping.

Yeah, he should've pushed Keith to push him harder before he left, should've asked for what he really needed. But it had been good no matter what—always was—and neither man had gotten any sleep.

It also didn't help that he'd had the feeling of being watched for a few days. The concept of the wilderness of mirrors was something that operatives dealt with—they were always on guard, suspicious, and therefore they found suspicion in every situation, warranted or not. He was pretty sure that was all this was, but he couldn't shake the nag.

He made a mental note to patrol the outside once the storm cut the area some slack. For now, he had to block everything out of his mind but Keith and his mission. Because even when they were separated, the man always counted on him. Reed wouldn't have it any other way.

8

Shane knew instantly that Keith was gone. The big man's presence was easily missed in the cabin, and he could tell Reed felt the loss keenly as well. At first, Shane didn't ask about it and then, as they had dinner Reed had cooked— stew and fresh bread he said had been dropped off by the delivery service earlier in the day—he'd said, "Keith's not coming back tonight?"

"Not tonight, no," Reed said. "Have more stew."

Shane had. There was tension in the blond man's shoulders, and at first Shane had wondered if they'd had some kind of falling out. But he'd heard the phone call later that evening, and he'd deduced that Keith was out on a job. It was the terms Reed had used, the code he talked in, a mix of military and mercenary, and it made sense that these men would've continued doing what they did best in the privates ector.

He didn't want to hang out spying, and so he grabbed a sweatshirt Keith lent him weeks ago and dragged it on with the shorts he wore and padded into the small office. Keith was usually the one behind the chair, muttering over the computer, handling the phone calls, so it was weird seeing Reed there instead.

Reed stopped typing and looked up at him. "I guess you're wondering where Keith is?"

"I heard you talking before. I'm guessing you guys do some private contracting on the side."

"How very PC of you, Shane." Reed cracked the first smile of the night. "We still like the term mercenary, but really, we're just happy to still be working."

"Mind if I hang out in here for a while?"

"Sure. I'll be camped out here for the next couple of days, so I was going to ask you to do a little cooking, if you're up to it."

"I am, no problem. But you're not going to sleep?" he asked.

"Not for the next forty-eight hours at least, no. Maybe quick naps here and there. But when Keith's on a job, so am I."

Shane appreciated that. "If it's okay, I'd like to stay up with you."

"You can try, but I'm not sure your stamina's up to it. Still, I'd like the company, even if you do start to snore."

It was true—Shane wouldn't make it up for much longer, not with the heavy dinner and the illness still lingering. The coughing fits were fewer and far between but too much activity still got him hacking like an old smoker. He'd just talked Reed into letting him work out a little with some of the lighter weights, but the only cardio he'd been allowed to do was the outside walking. And that was slow going.

He sat on the couch. One minute he was watching the news, the next, blinking himself awake while standing. Ever since his time in the Army, he stood first and woke second.

When he woke, he wasn't sure how much time had passed. He smiled sheepishly when Reed chuckled.

"Need some coffee?" Shane asked.

"That would be great, actually," he told Shane, who went to the kitchen to brew a fresh pot. Because although Reed's cooking was pretty good, his coffee was god-awful.

"And don't think I don't know you're throwing out the pot I made," Reed called and then muttered, "You and Keith both think you're the goddamned coffee kings."

Shane smiled and started the new pot to brew before strolling back to Reed. "Do I get to know more about the job he's doing?"

Reed considered that for a long moment before telling him, "It's outside the scope of what the military or alphabet agencies are allowed to do."

Code for negotiating with terrorists. Except he had a feeling that Keith wasn't the type to negotiate, but rather he'd blast his way in and take back what he came for.

It made him long for the days when he was actively doing similar tasks. He wondered how soon he'd be up for that and if he'd actually ever be in the game again. It was the first time he'd thought about that possibility in months, and he took that as a good sign.

"Lots of cream and sugar," Reed called as Shane went to grab the coffee. He grinned, since he took it the same way. Kyle used to tell him he took a side of coffee with his sugar. Basically, he used a shitload of the stuff in both their large mugs and brought them both back into the office.

Reed accepted his with a grateful look in his eyes before turning his full attention back to the computer. For a long while, there was just typing and then silence. Reed downed half the mug on the first try.

"Fruit of the gods," he said. "Nice and strong. I'll be up for days."

"This shit knocks me out better than pain meds," Shane admitted. "Then why drink it?"

"I keep hoping for different results."

"Which is, of course, the definition of insanity."

"If the shoe fits," Shane murmured as he took a sip. "I make good coffee."

Reed gave him a half grin after he'd taken a gulp of his. "Yeah, yeah, it can be your job from now on."

"Awesome. Hope it pays well." The word "well" caught on his yawn, which morphed into two more. He took another couple of sips before he put it down and wrapped the blanket around himself. *Just going to close my eyes for a second*, he lied to himself.

He swore he heard Reed laugh at him, even though he

hadn't spoken out loud. Swore he felt the blond man's hand on his cheek, too, but that might've been even more wishful thinking.

Keith caught some shut-eye on the jet that took him from Washington into the insertion point in the jungles of South America, near one of the British Embassies. His pilots were Trace and Gary, both former Air Force, who could put down planes on boats in the middle of the ocean with ease. These trips were cakewalks for them, but they were no less vigilant.

He went over the papers Prophet gave him this morning, getting familiar with the maps of the area and the like. He and Proph were supposed to meet up at the airstrip but Proph got busy with something and couldn't show. It was all right—the man always gave him more than enough intel to complete the job. The visits were extra, the friendship they'd developed over the years always intact.

The embassy layout was perfect—had a bottom layer of catacombs that were closed off from the top floors by wooden boards—nothing permanent, and also no security cameras, because in order to get inside, you had to dig a tunnel—or find one that was hidden and jump down six feet. It would be easy enough for him to get in that way, but there was no way he could take the mother and young son back that way.

He scratched his chin thoughtfully as he studied all the options, then put his head back and took a nap. For him, sleep always equaled the answer. He had to feed all the information into his mind and then he'd sleep and wake up with the solution.

He wished he could do that with Shane, but there was a distinct lack of information about the young man—and a great deal of confusion. But he brushed him from his mind now, put his head back and rested as the jet sped along to their destination under the cover of night, the flight plan only known to a select group of people.

When he opened his eyes an hour later, he began writing out his map, drawing what he needed to. Plotting the times along with coordinates, plus the equipment he'd be taking in. He'd share it with his back-up, who'd been asleep the entire flight, having just worked two back-to-back jobs for Prophet. Mick was former Army, a big guy with an impressive record as a solider and a more impressive one as a mercy. This was his element and, like Prophet, the man thrived under the lack of supervision.

Ten hours later, they were on the ground in a remote field. Keith would be walking in—Mick would wait at the halfway point. This part of the op would take about four hours, a conservative estimate if things went as planned.

He humped it through the jungle, NVs in place, his rifle at the ready, his mental compass guiding him toward the embassy. It had been deserted for well over a year, since a bombing and renovations had begun months ago. But the kidnappers had holed up in there three days ago, doling out their ransom demands that fell on deaf ears. At least that was the government's party line. In reality, they called to Prophet who ran Butler's teams, filled with mercs and dropouts from the CIA and random other men and women, to get those hostages out. Prophet's idea of negotiation was: we're taking the hostages and shooting you.

Keith agreed with those tactics.

He stuck to his plan, entering the catacombs, moving easily through the wooden boards that had been damaged with the original bombing and creeping silently into the middle room where he'd used his heat sensors to find the people.

Three kidnappers, plus the mom and kid in one room. Two men in the hallway. No men outside. He wondered why, had to assume the front and back doors and paths were booby trapped and cursed silently. A pain in the ass, but not a deal-breaker. Not when a woman and child's life were on the line.

He heard the boy crying as he got closer. His stomach tightened and he shoved his temper down where it belonged, along with any other emotions. He moved forward, took out the first guard almost silently, a knife to the carotid and a clean catch so he could place the body on the floor. The second guard came when he heard the gurgled cry and got the same treatment.

Now, to draw out the others, away from the mom and kid. It seemed like mom would be the type who could handle a gun—at least a handgun, and he would slide her one while he fought the others.

It was the best chance they had. He slammed the door open with his foot, knocking one out and letting the gun slide across the floor to the mom. Thankfully, the woman knew exactly what to do—he figured anyone living in this country knew how to handle a firearm and then some. She pushed her son behind her and held the gun out as he disarmed the two other men and killed them, because they couldn't afford for them to come after them as they made their escape.

"We're going to have to go back out through the catacombs," he told them, and they followed him quickly down the stairs. He stopped them before they went through. "Are either of you hurt?"

Because in these jungles, wounds got ugly fast.

"No, they didn't hurt us. I'm Sarah—this is Kevin."

"Keith." He shook her hand. "I'm going to get you both home."

She nodded and squeezed her son's shoulder. "We'll do whatever you say."

And they did, followed him fast through the underground, climbed out of the big hole and into the jungle with nary a complaint. Halfway through the walk, Keith picked the boy up and slung him over his shoulder so no branches would catch his face, told him to hang on and they picked up the pace.

It was too damned easy. And whenever things went this well, they went tits up just as fast. But he had the boy on his back and the mom holding his belt and keeping up and he just kept marching forward. Because that was his goddamned motto in life, keep marching forward and leave the other shit behind.

Until he had to break course and head in the other direction, thanks to a band of soldiers roaming the jungles. Whether or not they were searching for him or others, it made no difference. He'd quickly become a target.

He sent out a distress message to Mick, knowing that Reed would get it as well. These were the times he depended on them to get him the hell out of the jungle.

Shane was on his feet in front of the desk where Reed sat before he'd fully woken up. He remained there, dazed, swaying, the blanket falling off his shoulders as he stretched to shake the sleep off him. He blinked a few times, yawned a few more and rubbed his cheeks with his palms.

Reed grinned at him. "Old military habits die hard."

"Tell me about it." He massaged the back of his neck, stiff from the way he'd slept. "I guess I abandoned you."

"Not really. Nice to have another warm body in the room, no matter the state of consciousness." Reed bit his bottom lip as he typed something and then moved closer to the screen. "There's still some coffee left."

"I'll stick with soda."

"I'll take one," Reed said. Shane padded to the kitchen, grabbed a couple of Cokes and some Twinkies and headed back into the office. The fire was still going strong in the living room, and outside, the storm was definitely picking up. Pretty soon, the porch would be completely covered again, much the way it had been when he'd stumbled literally over it and landed with a bang against the front door.

He handed Reed a soda and tried to hold on to the cakes possessively, but Reed grabbed one for himself, gave Shane a smirk. "I hid the chocolate."

"I found it and rehid it," he said, and Reed's face furrowed into a frown. "You can't fuck with a man's vices like that," he muttered, and Shane ignored him in favor of stuffing the golden sponge cake that would survive any nuclear attack into his mouth.

He wanted to walk to the other side of the desk and take a look at things for himself, but didn't want to be all that presumptuous.

"What's he doing?" he asked instead around a mouthful of Twinkie. When Reed just stared at him, he washed it down with the cold soda before continuing, "I mean, can you tell me anything more specific?"

"Freeing hostages," Reed said. "How many?"

"A mom and her son. Dad's a diplomat."

"So they're collateral for the rebels in return for what, a vote?"

"Something like that." Reed handed him a file folder and Shane flipped through, his stomach churning as he read along.

"Keith's in real danger."

"Always."

"And he's alone?"

"For this part. Force Recon, remember? He can take on the world." But he was worried too, just refusing to admit it. "He carries a chip so I can track his movements."

"Do you guys ever go on missions together?"

"All the time."

He opened his mouth to ask, why not this time, but he knew and that sat like a rock in his stomach. He went to stand up, not sure where to go when Reed's hand came down on his forearm.

"Yeah, we split up this time because you're here and you need someone to take care of you. And don't give me that pissed-off look because you know it's true. It's not a big deal. We don't do every job together and neither of us minded Keith flying solo on this one."

"I'll bet Keith minded."

"Maybe a little more than I did," Reed admitted with a slight twist of his lip. "But he'll get over it."

Shane swallowed hard, trying to reconcile the two sides

of the Marine he'd seen so far. Tough-guy asshole and gentle, let-me-touch-your-face guy. Then again, Shane wasn't exactly one who could complain about hiding things from strangers.

But these two men had become the farthest thing from strangers in a short amount of time. And he sat there on the couch and listened to music and thumbed through a week's worth of newspapers idly as Reed traced Keith's movements. It went on for hours and Shane refused to leave or sleep again, because he'd become invested when he'd promised himself he wouldn't. This was one stop of many, and he had to move on.

Except he wasn't pushing to leave and they weren't exactly showing him the door.

Suddenly, Reed's entire demeanor changed. It would be impossible to tell for the most part, but Shane wasn't most people.

"What's wrong?"

Reed shook his head and typed, then started pulling out books and looking through them. Shane fisted his hands so hard his nails bit into his skin, forced himself to breathe calmly, not to bother Reed when he was obviously working through something major.

But… "Reed, let me help. I can help."

Reed looked at him for a moment, narrowed his eyes as if assessing that fact and then nodded.

"Take this." Reed handed him an iPad. "Try to find me a

recent map," he added as he rattled off coordinates.

Shane recognized the numbers almost immediately but pulled the map of the country up anyway. "Got it."

"I need a way out that doesn't include the water."

He stared atthe map, hyper-focusedon the area Keith was currently in.

Probably hiding in the jungles behind the embassy. "Is he moving west?"

"Yes, toward the bridge."

"There's no bridge there," Shane told him. "There's a bridge."

"There's not," he insisted.

Reed looked at him. "When's the last time you were in country?"

"Seven months ago. I blew up the fucking bridge."

Reed blew out a long breath, cursed and muttered something along the lines of, "You win."

"Tell him if he goes through the road that branches away from the bridge— the one through the jungle—it'll lead out to a farm. It looks like it'll take you over a cliff but it doesn't." He held his breath, not wanting any more questions but wanting Keith to just get the hell out of there safely.

Reed typed. Then picked up a phone and barked to someone who Shane assumed wasn't Keith. The person on the other line cursed but Reed held to Shane's assertions and finally, he heard a grudging acceptance.

Reed hung up and tapped his fingers as they waited

through the silence. Shane estimated it would be at least fifteen minutes before they heard if Keith got through, especially if he'd been successful with the hostages.

"He's not traveling alone, right?" Shane couldn't help but break the silence to ask.

"No, he got the hostages out." Reed said.

That meant Keith's job was halfway done. It was going to be a long night. It was almost five in the morning now, but the storm raged in earnest and it would look black as night for most of the daylight hours anyway.

"It's always easier when you're the one in it, no matter how bad it is," he heard himself say. At least that had always been his experience.

Reed glanced up from the computer for a moment, his expression dark, his hand on his chin. "Not always, Shane." And then his expression shuttered again into the stoic soldier.

Shane let that sink in as he counted the seconds in his head while pretending to read the paper. Wasn't fooling Reed but he was sure Reed appreciated it. Even his toes ached from the tension of sitting so damned still and waiting and praying he was right. Because he couldn't have more deaths on hishead.

If you hadn't said anything, there could've been deaths too...

No matter what, he'd had to say something.

After what seemed like forever but was actually under

the time Shane figured Keith could hump it with civilians, Reed typed something and sighed. Said, "He's back at the LZ and just boarding the helo. He'll be home tomorrow morning, with anyluck."

Shane smiled and stretched. "You gonna sleep now?"

"Not until he's home," Reed told him.

9

Shane slept on and off for the next day and a half, woke when he heard the door, his old instincts beginning to kick in. Reed went past him, giving him a light touch to his shoulder, letting him know he'd seen Shane stir.

Shane wasn't sure if he'd be intruding on a private moment but couldn't help himself. Even coming from the most successful mission, decompression was necessary and Shane wondered how Keith would act.

He wrapped the blanket around him to ward off the cold that always hit the body after two in the morning, no matter how many layers you wore. He watched Reed embrace the returning Marine, who'd set his bags down to return the hug.

Now, he was whispering something to Reed, his face intense, but then Reed laughed and Keith's eyes met Shane's.

"Hey," was all he could think of, and Keith nodded. Didn't seem angry, just not completely back yet. But he looked completely content in Reed's arms, and Shane felt a sharp pang of jealousy hit him…and he wasn't sure at first which one he was jealous of.

He realized it was both…and neither. He wanted to join both of them, not get in between them. And that revelation made his head throb.

"Shane, you look a little pale," Keith said, and Shane cursed himself for ruining their moment.

"No, stay. I'm fine. Keep…ah, doing what you're doing," he assured them, slipped back into the office and sat on the couch.

He heard their whispers, wondered if they were conferring about him or going about their other business of reuniting. He hoped for the latter, he thought as he lay curled on the cool leather, because he liked being in here, had come to think of it as the war room.

That was a place he was used to.

You almost gave away your hand, he reminded himself. Would have to be more careful from here on out. When he was sick, he wasn't talking, helping these men. But now that he was on the mend, the urge to do shit, to get back to his former self, before Kyle, was taking over.

Reed let Keith eat before insisting on checking him over. He knew the company who hired them had someone do that anyway as part of the mission protocol, but Reed always double-checked. Keith always grumbled, but conceded, mainly because he knew it was easier than arguing.

He found contusions, scratches, all expected. He'd already been put on a heavy-duty antibiotic, since jungles and infections did not mix.

"Gonna clear me, Doc?" Keith asked finally, his hands circling Reed's wrists as Reed looked down at him. They'd done the impromptu exam in the kitchen and were still conscious that Shane was close.

"You might have to try a little harder to get me to sign off on you," Reed told him now, and Keith raised a brow.

"You'll get it harder, if that's what you want," he said quietly, and Reed's body ached at those words.

He straddled Keith's lap, leaned in to him. "Missed you. So did Shane." Keith put his hands on Reed's hips and moved him back to glare a thim.

"Why are you pushing this?"

"Why are you resisting?"

"We don't know him."

"That's bullshit and you know it. Besides, he gives a shit about us."

"How do you know that?"

"He was trying to stay up while you were gone."

"You let him track me?"

"Come on, Keith, you know I'd never put you in danger." Reed paused. "But he was the one who told me about the bridge and the road."

Keith glared at him.

"I had no reason not to trust him."

"And no reason to trust him. Come on, Reed, there's more to this than meets the eye."

"Like what? He was a Ranger. It's perfectly logical that he would've been in the area blowing shit up seven months ago."

"He was discharged eight months ago," Keith bit out.

"So he got some dates mixed up. We've all done that—it's hard to remember timing in combat situation, and blowing up a bridge counts."

"Someone's mixed up, for sure."

"Ah, fuck you. And I know you won't admit it, but the bridge was gone, right?" Reed shoved his boots on and headed outside, needing to clear his head. Keith followed in short order, shutting the door behind him, the howl of the wind giving them some much-needed privacy.

"Reed, we've got to cut him off. We don't know him, don't know what he's capable of. Just because he was right about a bridge…"

"Don't tell me you're scared of him? Big, strong Marine like yourself?" Reed shot back and knew he was pushing it. But that was the only way to get Keith to accept anything—Reed's head hurt from the amount of times he had to be the battering ram at Keith's door.

And he always won—always.

He wasn't wrong when he'd showed up at the door eight years earlier, to find Bobby and Keith inside, sharing dinner and watching TV. Wasn't wrong when he'd stripped for them and let them fuck him, sandwiching himself between their bodies and the soft cotton sheets that had been like heaven.

He'd come home—he'd known that. And he wasn't about to let Shane walk away—or have Keith push him out.

"I'm not scared—I'm sensible. This kid has been through hell. Combat. I think you remember what that's like," Keith challenged, but his eyes had glazed for a second, that faraway place that signaled he was thinking of his time in and the things he'd seen and done. Reed knew he'd recognized the PTSD in Shane for sure…which meant he'd also know they were the best ones to help him. "You're too fucking impulsive, Reed."

"And you usually like it." He was spiraling—fast. He and Keith had been having sex—quiet sex—since Shane had arrived, and it had been barely enough to pull him back from the edge. He needed—wanted—craved more. And Keith could give it to him.

As much as he resisted—and he would really, truly resist—he would know, in the aftermath, that it was the right thing. He'd discovered it the first time Keith and Bobby had taken him in hand and showed him that he could find some peace through submitting to two dominating men.

"I am going to fuck that stubbornness right out of you." Keith spoke the words quietly, but they echoed in Reed's ears despite the storm.

"You can try," Reed told him. "But maybe I'll fuck you first."

Keith went after him, but Reed was ready. They crashed

through the door, Reed barely able to close it behind him, thanks to the wind, before Keith was ripping at his clothes and pushing him toward the bedroom at the same time.

"Shane is—" he started, but Keith cut him off, his voice low and dangerous. "Should've thought of that before you started with me. Maybe next time you'll learn your lesson."

"I've learned plenty," Reed spat at him as Keith shoved him into the bedroom. Reed's jeans were down around his ankles and he tripped his way into the room. The door caught on the rug, closed most of the way but Reed couldn't worry about that now. His mind reeled and survival instincts gripped him tightly.

He heard himself practically wheeze, even as Keith caught him and yanked at the wet jeans with no finesse. Reed ripped Keith's shirt off and broke the zipper on the big man's jeans as well. He'd give as good as he got.

But even though he knew the inevitable would happen tonight—that Keith would win and Reed would end up with Keith's cock buried deep inside him— Reed still fought. Tonight, for some reason, that was important.

He'd topped Keith before—not often—not nearly as often as Bobby had been allowed to, but it all somehow worked—three pieces of a seamless puzzle when they fell into bed, nuzzling and sucking and fucking until they couldn't come anymore.

Reed remembered coming home late some nights from a house call to find Bobby and Keith tangled in the bed or heard them fucking against the kitchen counters.

Sometimes, it was so fucking hot all he had to do was watch for a few minutes and he'd come hard in his pants. Like a wet dream without the sleep.

Sometimes, more often than not, he'd join them, end up pulled between the two powerful men, commanded and obeying like the good soldier he'd once been.

The Army had put him through college and med school, and had given him a wicked case of PTSD as a partinggift.

Bobby and Keith had eased all his burdens.

"You gonna calm down now?" Keith asked, backing off a little. Reed was naked, Keith just about there, and for a long moment, there was a standoff. Reed could get out of this.

Now, he slammed Keith, who fell back, surprised. But that didn't matter—he was up again, taking Reed to the ground. Ripping what was left of his soaked shirt off in a frenzy and rock hard, the way Reed had been since the argument began. Not giving a shit that they weren't alone in the house, because they were both beyond that.

"Remember, you asked for this, the way you always do," Keith growled, smacking his ass several times until Reed felt himself backing into the hands, his face surely as red as his ass at this point. He didn't even bother to try to get away because the first smack gave him the pleasure and pain he craved. It calmed him, brought him right to the edge.

And then Keith stopped cold.

Fucker would make him beg for it. And he would do it,

because he wanted…needed. "Fill me, Keith…please…"

"Don't you move, Reed. This is my game now."

Keith's finger played along his ass as Reed swallowed hard. This would be torture—sweet and painful all at once. His skin was drying and he was shivering from that and Keith's touches and he heard himself groan. His fingers dug into the rug as he tried to be good, stay still. But he couldn't. He moved back, trying to get Keith's fingers deeper, and he was rewarded with several hard slaps to his ass.

"You could've just asked," Keith told him. But of course that would've been too easy, and Reed was anything but easy. He squeezed his eyes shut and let the pain from the slaps override everything else in his mind.

He opened them only when he was sure he could stay still under Keith's machinations. The man had two fingers inside him, twisted them, brushed his prostate, and he heard himself beg. It was a keening, needy sound, and he couldn't hold it back.

Keith must've taken pity on him, or else the bastard was too horny himself to wait, because soon the man's thick cock was brushing his hole.

"Going to fill you, Reed." As he spoke, he yanked on Reed's hair, forcing him up on his knees so his back was against Keith's chest. He circled Reed's cock, stroked it hard several times and then stopped.

"Bastard," he bit out and Keith laughed. "Just the way you like it."

"I'd like you to fuck me right now."

"You'd better say what I need to hear."

He wanted to do nothing of the sort. Had fought this from day goddamned one with both Bobby and Keith. But they'd worn him down in the most blissful way possible and now, Keith knew he needed it again.

His eyes burned with tears—he didn't want to be humiliated. Didn't always understand where these needs and wants came from. But he would get nothing without the words—Keith was a hardass when he needed to be.

When he opened his eyes, he knew something in the room had changed. Without turning to look, he realized that Shane was watching through the small opening.

Reed could feel the kid's gaze on him as surely as Keith's dick pressing his ass insistently. And if Shane wanted to see what he'd be getting, Reed was more than happy to give him access to the entire show.

10

Shane leaned against the doorjamb silently, not wanting to disturb the scene he'd almost walked in on. He'd heard the commotion and he'd forced himself up to make sure Guthrie hadn't found him. He had a knife he'd picked up from the desk where Reed must've left it earlier—Keith's lucky knife, Reed had called it— and now, he let his hand drop to his side as he tried to control his breathing.

Because the scene in front of him was nothing like he'd expected.

Keith and Reed. Naked. On the floor, obviously having just come in from the outside storm, their wet clothing strewn in a path that led from the front door to where they currently lay.

They looked more like they were wrestling than fucking—Shane supposed that's how it was with those two anyway—a fight to dominate one another—this time with Keith ultimately winning.

What did Keith want Reed to say? He could see the words nearly forming on Reed's lips, but there was a stubbornness inside of that man that burned brightly.

"Reed, you need to say the goddamned words."

"I need you to fuck me and then spank me."

The words came out in a rush and Keith smiled and took no time at all to prove his dominance.

Shane's cock grew impossibly hard as he watched Keith pin Reed down on all fours and bite the man on the back of the neck—a show of the ultimate alpha, all while his cock pistoned in and out of Reed's ass.

Reed's face contorted—the line between pleasure and pain Shane longed for—and he found himself shoving his hands down his sweatpants and fisting his own cock in response, barely able to hold back his own moan.

Keith and Reed were loud enough that it wouldn't have mattered. Thought he was safely tucked away, out of earshot.

"You like that, don't you, baby?" Keith asked and when Reed didn't say anything, he tugged the other man's hair, bringing his head up. "I don't hear you."

"Fuck you."

"That what I'm doing to you, baby. And you love it— love when I fuck you this hard."

It took a while before Reed gave in again—Keith slammed his prostate until Reed's mouth hung open, his hands fisted on the rug in front of him, until he finally cried out, "Yes, Keith—you know…just fuck me—please don't stop fucking me."

Keith smiled then—and Shane thought it was the most beautiful smile he'd ever seen. Because, until that point, Keith had scared him—and Shane was a man used to violence. Now it seemed like Reed really did need this—the look on his face was pure heaven.

Suddenly, without a second of warning, Keith's gaze caught on him. Shane froze, hand on his exposed cock, mouth opened with impending orgasm, and waited.

Keith didn't stop what he was doing. If anything, he began to pump into Reed harder, grabbing his hips and drawing him closer, staring at Shane the entire time.

"You like that, don't you?" he asked, and Reed moaned in response, but Shane knew he wasn't talking to Reed at all. And so he nodded and began stroking his cock again, his body relaxed against the door, his eyes glued to Keith's.

"You've been thinking about this all day—all night—wanting it. Ready to open your ass to me," Keith continued and Reed was pretty much incoherent by this point, barely able to hang on to anything because he was being filled so hard—and so good, and again Shane nodded his consent, pictured himself in Reed's spot, with Keith pounding him...

And that made him start. Picturing himself as submissive to a powerful, dominant man—spread and fucked and pleasured next to Reed until the three of them couldn't stand anymore.

"Come, right now," Keith commanded, and Reed's moan was a keening acquiescence, as though it was happening against his will. Shane's cock spurted as he fisted harder, the orgasms tightening his balls, come shooting along his stomach and chest as he tried to keep his sweat-slicked body upright.

Shane came at the same time Reed did. Keith swelled with pride for a second, watching his two boys enjoy themselves. It had been a long time since he'd fucked Reed like this and not felt the cloak of guilt from losing Bobby seep into the action.

Nothing wrong with thinking of Bobby, but Bobby himself would have kicked Keith's and Reed's asses for mourning him so somberly and for so long.

Now, Keith pumped himself harder, his eyes locked to Shane's as the boy remained on shaky legs.

And then he let loose, came hard inside Reed, since they'd long ago given up condoms. Reed's tight ass milked his dick, and Keith rode out the climax, enjoying the feel of Shane's eyes on him.

Finally, he stared at the boy again. Shane was no doubt wondering if Keith would follow through on what he'd promised.

He wouldn't be disappointed. Neither would Reed.

"You're going to count," he told Reed now as he prepared, grabbing the paddle from the drawer in the nightstand. It was beautiful polished soft black leather on both sides, and it stung like a bitch. "Say it."

"I'm going to count." Reed's voice was still strangled from the orgasm and Keith gave him the first shot without warning. "One."

Keith continued, watching Reed's ass turn a beautiful shade of pink and then red, heard his voice grow drowsier and more content with each smack, until they reached twenty and the spanking was over. Reed's body, which had been drawn like a tight bow after his first orgasm sagged as he came on the last spank. He fell forward on his elbows and Keith put a strong arm around his waist to keep him up. Bent and kissed the back of his neck where he'd bitten the blond man earlier, and he swore he heard a soft moan from Shane float over them like the caress of a hand.

If they fucked Shane, they'd have to go back to condoms for a while. If they fucked Shane... Jesus, where the hell was this coming from? When he looked up again, the boy was gone.

"It turned you on that he was watching." Reed's words were casual as he leaned across Keith to grab a cigarette, lit it and blew a stream of smoke toward the ceiling before moving back down to the rug.

Keith had been lying on his back, staring at the ceiling, the orgasm having thoroughly ravaged him. "You knew Shane was there?"

Reed's mouth tugged slightly to one side. "Yeah, I knew—a while before you did. You forget, that was me, watching you and Bobby…wishing it could be me, you and him."

Keith cursed roughly and pushed up off the floor. "Fuck you, Reed. I know what you're doing. But we don't know anything—don't even know if he's interested."

"Yeah, okay." Reed took another long pull on the cigarette. "I'm pretty well willing to bet that if he jerked himself while watching us, he is."

"I'm not doing this." Keith tried to move away but Reed was up and on him in seconds—man moved like a cat when he wanted to. "Why are you pushing him away? He wants us. And you want him, if the way my ass feels is any indication."

Keith stuck his chin out. "What—I'm suddenly not enough cock for you?"

Reed smiled then, reached out and touched Keith's cheek, even when Keith tried to turn away. "Is that what this is about? You think that I need more?"

Keith shrugged. "We said, after Bobby…"

"We were in mourning. Bobby kept telling us that we would find someone else. And if that person never came, I'd sure as hell just be happy with the two of us. But the boy has come here, Keith. And Jesus, it's like seeing myself. I know what he wants—what he needs—and that's us. And if we're the ones who are supposed to make him happy—to protect him—well, I'm thinking that can only strengthen what we have between us."

"You feel this way because he showed up like you."

"And you think that doesn't mean anything?" Reed asked. "I'm trying not to think about it."

"You're the one who believes in signs."

"Fuck. I never expected...not like this."

"I wasn't looking either. You know that."

Keith did. But Shane coming had shifted the balance just by being him. There was no denying it. "You've barely talked to him. How do you know this is something you want, never mind what he wants?"

"Come on, man. You know as well as I do that we didn't speak—or even like each other much—before you fucked me."

Reed was one hundred percent correct. They'd connected through fucking and lying next to Shane on the floor while warming him up had made them realize what they'd been missing. It was a revelation, maybe a wake-up call that they'd been in mourning for too long.

"Just because we told Bobby we'd look—"

"Doesn't mean we have to accept the first gay man who passed out at our door," Reed finished.

Keith had been trying not to notice anything about Shane. But he knew he could get hard again just thinking about the way Shane looked when he came. "Just be careful."

"You're not going to try to get to know him?"

"Doesn't mean you can't."

Reed sighed, stared up at the ceiling. He might've needed tonight badly, but that didn't mean Keith didn't need something too and Reed wasn't sure how to go about giving it to him, felt as helpless as goddamned hell.

As if seeking to calm him, Keith reached out and rolled him so Reed was trapped. "I thought I fucked the thinking out of you."

"Ninety percent," Reed told him. "If you're up for the other ten?"

"For you, always."

Reed was sore from earlier, but it was the best kind of sore. Keith's cock eased into his ass, the man had his thrust perfected and Reed locked his ankles around the man's back and let himself be taken—claimed—again.

Keith liked face-to-face fucking the best. Reed could only enjoy it after something like the sex and the spanking that had happened previously. Now, he felt like he was flying as Keith rocked against him, his cock hitting the gland that make Reed cry out.

He'd never been loud during sex before Keith. Even with Bobby, he tended to be quieter when it had been the two of them. But when Keith was near, he touched something primal within Reed—and Reed appreciated that with his vocalness.

Keith didn't mind—his dark eyes glowed as Reed called his name in between other things like fuck and hurry and oh yeah, right goddamned there.

Reed's body tightened, balls hard and close to his body, but he wanted to prolong this, the sensation of climbing, flying…right here, this was perfection. He stared up at Keith and Keith smiled down at him, his expression one of near bliss. His cock filled Reed until he didn't think he could stand it another minute.

"Love you," he managed. He clung to the man as the rhythm sped up, until the bed creaked under their movement and the floor shook under it.

"Beautiful baby," Keith murmured into his ear, and that was it. Reed roared to a climax with Keith's words, the name he'd given Reed within the first weeks of meeting him.

The first night that Keith had called him beautiful boy, the night Keith had really shown Reed what he needed started innocently enough. Reed had slept with Bobby a few times with Keith there, but the man had somehow managed to keep his distance when he joined them. Spent more time with Bobby than Reed, and Reed hadn't liked that at all, just couldn't figure out why, because Keith made him nervous as anything.

He'd been there for two months and Keith had never approached him when he was alone, although they'd had opportunities. When Bobby was there, Reed always felt safe enough to push Keith with little digs about the Marines that he knew annoyed the big man.

That particular night, he'd spent dinnertime antagonizing

Keith, goading him with Marine insults and other jabs that he knew would get Keith riled up.

The more he tried to piss the Marine off, the calmer Keith got. And then Bobby went out unexpectedly—and Reed found out later he'd left purposely because he knew what was going to happen—and at that point, Reed realized how badly he'd miscalculated.

He and Keith remained at the table, but Keith was suddenly staring at him like he was prey. Reed's stomach fluttered, like a fucking girl with butterflies, and he struggled to say something snide but no words came out. His throat was tight, mouth dry as Keith's hands tapped a drumbeat on the table.

Reed had escaped from a lot of men in his day—but he knew instinctively that there was no place to run far enough away from Keith. And still, instinct insisted he try.

He got as far as the guest room door before Keith was on him. He hadn't even heard the big man get up, had assumed—hoped—that Keith hadn't decided to follow him after all.

"You can dish it out, Reed—now it's time to see what exactly, you can take," Keith murmured against his ear as his body pressed Reed's to the still-closed door.

Reed wanted to tell him he could take anything a Marine could dish out, but he didn't think that was true. What was true was that his dick turned traitor, had been rock hard from the second the chase had started.

Maybe even a bit before that too.

"Keith, get your hands off me," he growled. "No."

Reed struggled but it was useless. He was highly trained and to this day he didn't know if it was because he was still recovering from nearly dying, or if he'd actually somehow let Keith win—and Keith would deny the latter—but Keith had him cuffed in seconds, but hands in front of him. Reed thought smugly that he could retaliate cuffed like that, but he'd been so damned wrong.

Keith dragged him over to a chair in the living room, had Reed flipped over his lap, pants down, trapping his legs. "You have pushed this as far as it can go, boy."

"Fuck you," Reed spat in lieu of anything more coherent because his brain turned hot with panic. He shuddered when Keith chuckled and said, "Later, I'm going to fuck you. For right now, you're going to find out who's in charge here."

"No one's in charge of me."

"You definitely need someone to take you in hand," Keith said. "I'm the one to do it."

Reed had been about to make a snide comment but realized how completely, utterly trapped he was. But before the panic could truly set in, Keith's hand came down on his ass. Hard.

He cried out, a combination of surprise, anger and pain. The slaps that followed weren't gentle, had Reed squirming and then yelling and finally, he realized how rock hard he still was. How much his body was responding to the perfectly timed blows Keith peppered onto him until finally the cacophony in his head stopped and there was blissful, peaceful silence and a matching pleasure he'd never felt before.

His body jackknifed without warning and he came. Didn't recall much beyond a blinding white light behind his eyes, heard himself crying out, and he didn't know how long he remained like that, but was pretty sure he'd come hard enough to make himself pass out.

Finally, when he stirred, Keith allowed him to slide to the floor. He remained on his knees, half afraid to look up, tears streaming his cheeks. Mainly because he was worried that Keith would laugh at him, tell him to get out. Tell him that he could never again experience that feeling because now that he'd been found, he never wanted to be lost again.

When he finally gained the courage to meet Keith's eyes, he noted that the man had been watching him, waiting patiently. When he spoke, his voice was firm but his eyes were kind.

"Do you always make things so difficult for yourself?"

"Yeah," he said in a rough, raw voice.

"Well, now you know what you've been looking for." Keith reached forward and ran a hand through Reed's hair. When Reed started to cry again, Keith dropped to his knees and held him tight. "I've got you."

"How the hell did you know?"

"I had a similar experience."

"I can't see you submitting to anyone."

"Sometimes. Less than before, but I've learned that if you need it, it's best not to fight it. You were worried I'd think you were weak or crazy. So you pushed me into the punishment."

Reed nodded at the truth. "I don't think I'm done."

"Not by a long shot," Keith agreed. "On the bed. Hands and knees, ass in the air."

Reed scrambled to do so, because suddenly nothing was more important than pleasing this man. With his ass spread wide to him, Reed buried his head in the comforter and Keith's cool hands touched his abused ass, rubbed the cheeks lightly. And then he'd buried his face into Reed's ass and tongued him, licked him, ate him until Reed was screaming into the comforter, barely able to control himself.

He humped the sheets, cock aching for another release, and Keith hadn't stopped him or told him he couldn't come. But something inside him needed— wanted—craved the command, and when Keith ordered him to come, he climaxed with a hard curse and shot all over the sheets.

Now, Keith was telling him, "I've got you," and Reed was pulled from his reverie.

"Sorry, I was just…"

"Yeah, I figured." Keith gave him that all-knowing look and rubbed his hand along Reed's sore ass. "It's a damned good memory. And we have plenty of time to make more of them."

11

Shane had never been more turned on in his entire life. Was still hard after he spent time in the bathroom, cleaning off his stomach, wondering how he was going to face those men again.

He was sure Keith would tell Reed he'd watched them.

But Keith didn't seem to mind. Maybe Reed would. The last part of the scene had been so goddamned intimate. He'd never known something like that could be. And as he stroked himself to completion a third time, thinking of the look on Reed's face, the way Keith's hand must feel, he came in a quiet, shuddering rush, barely hanging on to the side of the sink as he did.

He definitely needed a shower. The mirror showed him a week's growth of beard, pasty skin and bedhead. He ran the water hot and jumped into the large steam shower, letting the soap that smelled like Reed soothe him as he formulated his next move.

Feeling halfway human—and still embarrassed—he dried himself, went back into the room he was staying in and put on a pair of sweats and a T-shirt.

He heard more noises coming from Keith and Reed's room—a yell—and fuck, he hated himself for even thinking about spying again. Told himself he was simply checking to make sure the men weren't actually angry, that he hadn't misread the entire thing.

He had a feeling the whole fight had been about him anyway. But when he got close to the door, he heard softer sounds mixed with harsh breaths and his eyes filled.

He'd had that, this love the men had for each other, and now it was gone.

Maybe his loss hit him hard for the first time.

He was crying and he didn't care.

But he also didn't make it back to his room before he was discovered. To his absolute fucking horror, Keith found him first.

"Shane, are you hurt?" he asked, a hand on his shoulder, and Shane wished he could turn into that big chest for comfort. Hell, there was nothing to say he couldn't, but Keith wasn't exactly his biggest fan.

He did, however, check to see if he was wearing clothes. Sweatpants.

Disappointment curled in his chest.

What? Did you think he'd come out naked and invite you to join them?

That image flashed a second time in his mind. Maybe Reed had given him some weird drugs or maybe the fever was back. Or hell, maybe he just needed a drink.

"Sorry. Didn't mean to interrupt," he managed, tried to break Keith's grip as he kept moving away from their bedroom, but Keith stopped him once they got to the living room.

The fire still blazed and he was cold. He dropped down in front of it, because he was having a reaction to Keith touching him, couldn't face him, because Keith knew he'd watched. Knew he'd come.

He also gave up any pretense that he hadn't picked this exact moment to grieve, to miss Kyle and the life they might've had.

Reed was next to him moments later. Keith wrapped a blanket around his shivering form and Shane drew in a long, broken-sounding breath. Brushed tears from his face.

"Sorry," he said again. "It's just…I saw you and I was missing Kyle."

"Keith shoving me around on the floor and not letting me up reminded you of your relationship?" Reed asked, and Shane snorted in spite of everything.

"When it was quieter. Dammit, it's not like I go around watching guys fucking."

"We weren't exactly quiet. We didn't mean to do that with you in the house," Reed told him.

Shane finally met his eyes. "I wasn't honest with either of you. I was dishonorably discharged from the Army."

"What happened?" Reed asked.

"They accused me of stealing and selling munitions. A fucking lie." He heard the anger, the bitterness in his tone, saw Keith nod. "You knew all about this."

"We figured you'd tell us when you were ready," Reed explained, but Keith remained silent.

Shane couldn't, it seemed, for any longer. "Kyle was KIA a few months before the discharge."

But he would not elaborate on the connection between the two events. He'd revealed enough and embarrassed the shit out of himself.

"I bet you're starving," Keith said finally. "Come on—I'll make you something."

It had to be close to two in the morning, but his stomach didn't care. A good sign. He followed the men into the kitchen as Keith began to heat up and lay out leftovers.

Before he'd arrived here, it had been a while since he'd had anything close to resembling a home-cooked meal. He and Kyle never had much time for cooking.

"Here. Eat, don't think," Keith admonished as he pushed a food-laden plate in Shane's direction. It was the best order he'd heard in a while, and he had no doubt it was an order.

He did as Keith asked, noted the two men ate heartily as Keith checked the television weather to track the newest storm. According to the projections, it looked as if it would hover over them for the next twenty-four hours.

Hopefully, Guthrie hadn't been able to track him. When he'd first arrived in the area, he'd purposely followed the path of the Christmas Eve storm, hoping to disappear into it.

He'd almost succeeded in killing himself in the process, so job well done.

He sighed and Keith responded by spooning more meat and potatoes into his plate. Reed was already working on a big piece of chocolate cake.

"Why are you being so nice?" he asked before he could help himself. "I'm not nice," Keith said.

"I try to balance him out," Reed said with a grin as he finished his cake and grabbed the finished dishes and put them into the sink. "We'll deal with this tomorrow."

"Great. Mind if I watch TV for a while?" Shane asked.

"Reception's spotty but we can pop in a movie," Reed said. "I don't sleep all that much either."

He didn't elaborate on that, but in the military, you got used to going on less sleep than most. "I've slept enough for a lifetime."

"Not nearly. You're still recovering." Keith gave Reed a quick massage on his shoulders and told them to have fun, that he was hitting the sack.

"I don't want you to feel like you need to keep me company...especially if you'd rather, ah—"

"He needs his sleep after dealing with me tonight," Reed paused. "It must've looked—"

"Hot. It looked fucking hot."

"Yeah, that too. I probably should be embarrassed, but

I'm not. I learned a long time ago that what I need is what I need—it's no one else's to judge. So thanks for not doing that."

"How…?"

The question didn't come out but Reed understood. "How did I know that I needed that? I always felt like something was missing. When I was shown what that missing piece was, everything came together. So I'm always going to need it, but I found people willing to give it to me."

He pointed to the picture on the side table. Shane reached up for it, brought it down so he could see. It was in a simple dark wood frame.

"Who's this?" he asked.

Shane was pointing to the picture of Bobby, taken eight years earlier. The Bobby that both Reed and Keith liked to remember, not the skin-and-bones man who'd died of cancer last year.

Reed had seen Shane looking at the pictures before, but he'd never asked about them and Reed had never offered any explanation. Until now.

"Bobby. That was taken about three months after I met him and Keith." Reed took the picture from Shane and rubbed a finger over Bobby's chest. "He and Keith had been together for about six years before I got here. He died last year. Pancreatic cancer. He fought it for a long time because we wanted him to fight— and he did. But he stayed longer than he should have—for us. In the end, he finally told us, guys, please, I have to go…if you're ready. We'd been so fucking selfish."

He wiped his eyes viciously as Shane said, "Selfish? You took care of him."

"You've got it all wrong, Shane. Bobby took care of me. Just like Keith. And now Keith's got to deal with me all by himself."

"It doesn't seem like he minds at all," Shane said softly, and for the first time, Reed began to realize that the boy might just be right. "You mentioned that you lost someone too. Before Keith?"

"Actually, I met Bobby and Keith at the same time. I lived here with both of them."

"Like, together together?"

"I didn't expect it to happen either. Like I said, they'd been together for years before I showed up here, lost. Sick. Looking for the inn."

"Now you're freaking me out."

"It'll get worse if I tell you it was on Christmas Eve." Reed shrugged. "This place has always had the reputation of bringing people together who are meant to betogether."

Shane's mouth opened, then closed. He looked over at the picture again and Reed handed it to him. He stared down at it, like he was trying to figure it all out. Instead of saying anything else about the relationship, he said, "You got your degree in theArmy?"

"Yep. Bobby was a Marine, like Keith." He paused. "Have

you given any thoughts to your next steps?"

"I was going to see if some private firm would hire me, but with the dishonorable…" He trailed off. In reality, he'd only given it a passing thought, because he was so much more focused on staying alive and trying to prove Guthrie had framed him and killed Kyle. He wondered why they hadn't asked about brig time—maybe they'd just assumed it, or thought the charges hadn't stuck.

For the first time in months, he didn't feel like crying when he thought of Kyle's name. Instead, he leaned forward and he kissed Reed, felt the surprise in the other man. But Reed didn't pull away, let Shane come closer.

He took advantage of that, put his hands on either side of Reed's face and kissed him harder. The man tasted like whiskey and chocolate. He tasted like home…but this wasn't.

Shane pulled back. "I'm—"

"Don't be sorry if that's what you wanted. I'm not," Reed said. "But Keith—"

"You needed to kiss me. You needed comfort. That's something Keith understands." Reed stared at him. "You like it here."

"Yeah, I do. I like both of you. I felt it pretty quickly," he admitted.

"I felt it within the first two days I came into this place," Reed said. "Sometimes, you know exactly where you belong. Who's to say it can't be easy? It doesn't sound like anything else in your lifewas."

"I'm clean," Shane blurted out, and Reed nodded, asked, "Can I find your medical records somewhere?"

"The Army should have the last ones from six months ago. I haven't been with anyone since then. You'd have to go on my word."

"I don't know why you'd lie about that."

"I wouldn't. But I should go to bed," Shane whispered. "I should never have watched you guys."

"Did you imagine yourself in my place?" Reed asked.

"Between both of you," he admitted. Grabbed the bottle but Reed pushed it down, and for a long moment they stared at one another.

"Tell me more."

Reed could obviously be as commanding as Keith if called upon to do so. He swallowed. Had enough Dutch courage, so he said, "I want Keith's cock in my ass and you sucking me."

Reed's breath caught, but his eyes glowed. "What about the last part?"

"The spanking. I've never—"

"That's not what I asked, Shane."

"I'd let Keith spank me."

Reed kissed him this time, but it was on the back of his neck. It was soft, a brush of rough from his cheek. He shivered, his cock straining.

"Think you can sleep now?"

"Yes," he lied. Reed gave him a small smile and walked back to his bedroom where Keith was.

Shane knew he could stop him. Call him back and Reed could come. But he wasn't ready for all that would bring yet. Instead, he contented himself with smelling Reed on his skin.

12

Keith got in a couple hours sleep before the beep woke him. He glanced over to see Prophet pop up on FaceTime on the iPad.

"What's going on with Reed?" Proph demanded in that characteristic way of his.

"And he calls me a suspicious bastard," Keith muttered as he rolled his neck and tried to wake himself up a little more. "It's this Shane kid. He's invested." Proph's brow furrowed. "I told him about the dishonorable last month when Shane first got there."

"Reed's thinking he might've been framed."

"Maybe. There was a short stay in the brig but they couldn't make the charges stick. They gave him a dishonorable anyway and he didn't fight it," Proph mused.

"Shane told us about the discharge," Reed said quietly, and Keith nearly jumped through the ceiling.

"Fucker always does that," Prop said.

"Fuck you too," Reed said as he joined Keith against the pillows. "I know you're both worried about me."

Proph didn't bother denying it and Keith added, "There's something he's not telling us."

"I agree. I feel like he's mixed up in something."

"Like guns and warlords," Prophet piped in.

"He's running from more than a dishonorable discharge," Reed finished, choosing to ignore Prophet. Reed looked confident in what he was saying, and Keith had learned over their many years together that Reed's instincts could also be impeccable. It just wasn't often that they were at odds with Keith's.

Then again, Keith found himself more reluctant to let Shane in, as opposed to a concern in a bad, this-kid's-going-to-kill-us way. So maybe, just maybe, he and Reed were on the same goddamned page. "I think you need some separation. Maybe a job?" Prophet said.

Keith was surprised when Reed agreed with no reluctance. "Find me something and I'll go. If that's all right with you?" he asked Keith.

"Always is."

"You two kiss and make up. Or just kiss," Proph said and signed off.

Keith put down the iPad as Reed said, "If I go, can Shane stay? If he wants to."

"Do you think he'll want to stay here that long?"

"I don't think he's got a place to go. Correction—I think

he doesn't have a place to go and I think he's hiding."

Keith would have to look into the circumstances surrounding the Dishonorable Discharge more closely. "If you think he needs to stay, I'll give it a shot."

"I told him. About us. And Bobby."

"And?"

"He was surprised, but he recovered quickly. He's intrigued. Turned on. I think...I think he might be more like me than even I thought."

Keith took that into consideration. He'd never minded being the dominant one—the role came naturally to him. Taking care of Reed did as well...but there was something about Shane that made him think Reed might not be one hundred percent right. Still, he went along with it. "Which means..."

"He needs you more than he needs me." Reed whispered the admission as though he was ashamed to have needs at all. Keith grabbed him fiercely, rolled the blond man under him.

"I love your needs, dammit. Love you. Have from the goddamned moment you told me off when I tried to help you."

"Not love at first sight, huh?" Reed teased.

"Definitely not." Keith ground against him. "Lust, for sure."

"Yeah, it took you an entire twenty-four hours to fall in love with me."

"You were dying, Reed."

"Sometimes, I feel like I still am."

"I know," Keith said softly. "But it's happening less and less."

"He kissed me," Reed admitted.

"I'm not surprised." In truth, Keith had figured Reed would be fucking Shane in front of the fire, and maybe he wanted that. It would be easier for Reed to let Shane in first...but although Reed was the nicer of the two, he wanted Keith to be the one to make the first move alone. Needed it to work like that, more like the setup Reed walked into in the first place. "I wouldn't mind seeing it."

"Yeah, you just watching—that would be a first," Reed teased, then captured Keith's mouth in a slow, hot kiss. Like he was sharing Shane with Keith. Because that's exactly what Keith knew Reed wanted to do.

Shane stood in the hallway again, as unsure as he'd been since arriving. He couldn't tell these men the truth—not the whole truth, anyway. But if he admitted just enough to let them know what he'd been through, what they could be up against...

And what are you expecting in return?

The problem was, he couldn't answer that. Not yet, anyway.

He was good at pretending, at parceling out the truth

in increments when necessary, like he'd been doing with Keith and Reed. He'd been doing it for as long as he could remember. It made him a perfect candidate for the CIA. He'd been recruited for a job after less than six months in the military. He'd been handpicked by an undercover operative who'd worked with him, trained at Quantico. He'd leveraged that break to become one of the youngest operatives they'd ever trained and sent into the field. He'd gone back into the Army—to Ranger school—and he stayed undercover to ferret out Rangers who'd been using their rank to move munitions and sell them to rebels in third-world countries. Ultimately, that was what he'd been accused of doing himself, but that had been a lie.

He'd also broken a major rule. He'd fallen in love, had shown his hand. His fault. If he hadn't, Kyle would be alive and the right person would be in the ground.

You.

And again, he'd escaped death in the freezing temps. He'd saved himself because he'd fallen on a porch instead of the massive field to the right, and he had no idea what prompted him to walk in that direction in the first place. He'd fallen into a situation with two men who could see right through him…if he let them. And maybe, even if he didn't.

Shane knocked on the door, even though it was partially open. Keith was lying on top of Reed, heard, "You two are like fucking rabbits," come out of his mouth.

It made Reed laugh. Keith didn't, rolled off Reed and sat up, prepared to say something he would probably regret. But one look at the kid's face had him asking, "What's wrong?"

Shane looked at them and the bed and swallowed, hard. The kid didn't want to be alone—he could tell. But he wasn't ready to invite this kid into the bed, not in the sex way— they were all too goddamned vulnerable.

Still, he motioned for Shane to come in, patted the edge of the bed. He and Reed had clothes on and neither man was under the covers.

"I wasn't completely honest with you," Shane told Reed. "Well, with either of you."

"It's not easy talking about a dishonorable, especially if you think you were wronged," Reed told him, but Shane shook his head.

"I mean, yeah, I didn't do what I was accused of. But there's more to the story. And after I tell you…look, if you need me to go, I get it. But I can't keep lying to you. I should—and I don't know why I goddamned can't." His face flushed. "I was doing it to protect you guys."

Keith held back a laugh. It had been a hell of a long time since anyone so fresh-faced and young had worried about his safety. But he remained stoic, because he wanted to hear the kid out.

"Go ahead, Shane. I can pretty much promise you we can handle anything," Reed said.

"Kyle and I met in the Army. We weren't in the same company or anything, but still—it wasn't exactly something we shouted from the rooftops, repeal of DADT or not. We were in Afghanistan and I caught the tail end of a roadside bomb—enough to nearly shatter my eardrums and knock me on my ass. I was out of it, lying on my back, and Kyle was leaning over me and…" He paused, wiped an angry tear from his face and continued, "And someone shot Kyle from behind. And at first, I thought it was a rebel. But when I looked, I saw him. Guthrie. And there was no reason for him to be shooting at a member of his own team. We hadn't been under fire."

Reed had paled and Keith ran a hand across the back of his neck to bring him back from whatever terrible place he was headed to in his mind. To his credit, Reed shook it off immediately, as if knowing helping Shane was something that could actually help him as well.

"Did you report it?" Keith asked.

"I passed out. When I woke up in the hospital and they told me that I was being accused of selling guns to the rebels. They had evidence against me, thanks to Guthrie. When I told them I saw Guthrie shoot Kyle, it was my word against Guthrie's, and the range of Kyle's gunshot wound didn't match where I saw Guthrie aiming from."

"Is it possible that Guthrie heard the shot and broke position to check things out?" Keith asked.

"No, that's not the way it happened," Shane said quietly.

He'd left out a good chunk of what actually happened because he couldn't goddamned tell them classified information…

Bullshit. You don't want to tell them. You don't want to admit what happened.

But it didn't matter—the outcome was the same—Kyle was dead because of Guthrie and Guthrie was threatening him. Stalking him. And every day Shane got stronger, he was a day closer to stopping Guthrie from doing any more harm to him.

"You did brig time?"

"A month." He had, until the CIA got him cleared of charges. They kept the dishonorable discharge, didn't bother to fight it because Shane wasn't really in the Army anyway. "When they couldn't prove the gun charge, they released me and…" He rubbed his eyes hastily, in case some tears had fallen that he hadn't felt. "After that, I was just… dead inside. Kyle was…"

He paused, searching for the right words, the ones he was never able to find. Not until he came here and saw Reed and Keith and what they had between them. "Kyle was everything. Hell, I'd never even thought of letting anyone know I was gay until he kissed me one night after a drunken brawl we'd stumbled out of."

Keith remembered those days, when he'd been young and heady, ready to take on the world but unable to actually be himself. Not totally, anyway. He was a Marine through and through, like his daddy before him and his grandfather before that. But the gay thing…he'd known it since high school but hadn't come to terms with it until Bobby.

Bobby just brought it all to the forefront for him. There was something about a first love…

But that didn't mean that second or third loves weren't just as damned sweet or special. Sometimes, they were even more so, because you knew better, knew that you had to treasure the damned short time you had together. "He sounds like a good guy."

"The best. Maybe it sounds stupid, but I think…you would've really liked him."

"I'm sure I would've. He had good taste in men." Shane smiled shyly. "Thanks."

"And this Guthrie character—he's been after you?" Keith said.

"Yes. I know it sounds crazy, because he was cleared of any wrongdoing and I came out the loser in the case. He's retired and no one's been able to find him. It's like he fell off the map."

"Which is why the police don't believe you?"

"I didn't go to the police. I wanted to handle this on my own. Guthrie's after me. I can feel it. And if I don't leave—"

"You're not leaving," Reed said tightly. "Don't you even think about it." Before Shane could say anything more, the blond man left the room.

"He's okay. It's just…he doesn't want anything to happen

to you. And he doesn't want to lose you," Keith said.

"And what about you?" Shane asked. "What about me?"

"You're less…forgiving than Reed's been."

"That's true. You've got balls for saying it," Keith admitted. "I want to make sure you're all right, Shane. You've been through hell—and I think you're telling the truth."

"I…I wanted to join you," he admitted.

"You did," was all Keith said. "What else do you want? You've already kissed Reed."

Shane felt his face flush, looked at Keith who didn't look upset or worried. "I'm sorry."

"I didn't say you had to be sorry, dammit. I want to know what you need. I'm not in the habit of taking advantage of young men who pass out on my doorstep. It's one thing to be horny. It's another to be in trouble and not tell us," Keith finished, and Shane saw white.

"What the fuck do you want from me? I've been running for my life for the past six months. I lost my lover. I lost my career. I'm pissed off. Scared, and I have no one in the goddamned world to turn to," he told them. When he met Keith's gaze, there was a depth of understanding there he never would've expected.

"Yeah, you do," Keith told him. "You have two people to go to, and lucky for you, you're already here."

Reed came back in then, walked past him and patted the space in the middle of the bed. "Come here, Shane."

"I couldn't."

"Then we'll sleep in bed with you," Reed countered.

"You wake up screaming at night, but you calm down as soon as one of us touches you," Keith explained. "This is sleep only. No strings. Come on—we could all use a solid eight."

Crawling into the middle of these two men made him hard. He got on his stomach like that would solve anything. As soon as he did, both men touched him, an arm, a thigh brushing his.

"It'll help, Shane," Reed said sleepily. "Always helped me."

He was too tired to think about what that meant, but he swore he simply blinked and when he looked at the clock again, it was morning. He wouldn't have known that by the gray sky, heavy with the swell of another incoming storm, but the clock read ten in the morning. A solid eight.

He had to glance over Reed to see the clock. Reed had turned to face him, his arm and leg thrown casually over Shane's back. He felt the heat from Keith's body as the man's heavy thigh remained touching his.

And then the phone rang and both men were up and alert as if they hadn't just been in deep REM sleep. Keith took the call, handed it to Reed, who said, "You'd better grab me soon, before this storm hits," and hung up.

And then both men were staring at him. All he could think of to say was, "I don't think I screamed last night."

Reed and Keith blinked at him for a moment and then laughed.

"You might be the only man to spend a night in this bed who hasn't," Reed managed finally.

Shane grinned. He wouldn't mind giving up that record.

13

Spending the night with Shane between them was a way to ensure a quiet night—and a frustrating one. Touching the younger man only made him want to touch him more. Reed supposed Keith felt the same way, but it was good to see Shane sleeping peacefully.

He yawned a few times and figured he could catch a few quick naps on the flight to wherever Proph was sending him. Grabbed some gear from the attic space they kept it locked up in and carried it all downstairs to sort it out.

"You sure you're all right with this?" Keith asked him as he dumped the stuff onto the bed and mentally checked off the items on his must-bring list. Reed knew he'd wanted to ask it for hours now, but to his credit, held out the entire time he was making Reed breakfast, making Reed come in the shower—several times—and now, he was hovering.

He didn't do this normally, but nothing was normal these days. "Losing faith in me, hoss?"

"Never. I could go with you, if you need. I think Shane would be okay here, or we could ask someone to check in on him."

"You're worried about being alone with him."

"I don't know what's going to happen, Reed. If you were here, it'd be different."

"What are you worried about?" he asked, and Keith's expression tightened. "It's not being unfaithful to me or to Bobby. Not if I'm telling you to try it. Look, I didn't ask for this to happen, but it did. Shane fell into our laps. He's meant to be in our lives in one way or another. And he's sure as shit interested in you."

"In me?" Keith shook his head.

"Just let it happen. Whatever's meant to. It's the only way we're going to know for sure if this is right."

"I was planning on offering him a job, not sleeping with him."

Reed glanced up at the man's dark eyes and told him seriously, "You can do both."

Keith stared up at the ceiling for a second, shook his head and just said, "Ah Reed."

"I'm not blind—I have suspicions."

"But you've somehow let him in here." Keith tapped his hand over Reed's heart.

"And how often do I do that?" Reed asked pointedly and Keith conceded to the point with a nod. "And don't tell me you don't like him."

"I don't."

"You're lying."

"He's turning into a wise ass."

Reed shrugged. "So we're finally seeing the real Shane. Isn't that what you wanted all along?"

"Yeah, be careful what you wish for."

Shane lingered at the door as Reed packed. The bag looked innocuous enough, but based on the work the man did, Shane would lay bets as to the number of concealed weapons it contained, never mind the amount on his body.

He wore all black. A bandana wrapped around his head. And there was this look in his eyes that all soldiers got. Reed was already gone. His standing there in the flesh was merely a minor inconvenience to him that could be rectified easily by the private helo he'd be jumping on within the hour. In Reed's mind, the job—the battle—had started.

"I'll be back in a few days," Reed promised.

Shane didn't know what to say, even as *I'll miss you* and *I'm fucking nervous as hell to be alone with Keith* ran through his head.

Instead of saying any of that, he merely said, "Okay."

"Gonna give me something from you to come back to?" Reed asked. Keith was in the doorway, looking lazily between him and Reed.

Finally, Reed reached around and palmed the back of Shane's neck, pulled him in close and kissed the ever-loving shit out of him. A different kiss than the other night. This one wasn't tame, and Reed wasn't letting him pull away.

Instead, the man's tongue took his mouth hungrily, like

he was drowning and Shane was the water. He started to panic because Keith was there…Keith would get angry…

But then Keith's hand rested on the back of his head and that touch was gentle, calmed him enough to enjoy it. If Keith didn't mind…

Keith didn't mind. He put his arms around Reed, as if to stop him from moving away and Reed laughed softly into Shane's mouth. When he pulled back, he had a crooked smile on his face and he stroked Shane's cheek roughly.

"Beautiful. Fucking beautiful." His voice was rough. Shane figured that was the end of it, until Reed dropped to his knees. Shane shuddered at the sight of the man between his legs, but Keith was right behind him. He leaned against Keith as Reed unzipped his jeans and freed his cock, wasting no time in taking it inside his mouth.

"Holy fuck," Shane murmured. Couldn't deny it was what he'd wanted to happen last night when they were all lying on the bed together. But he'd understood why it hadn't.

His cock was encased in Reed's hot, wet mouth, the suction making Shane jolt. His hands curled in Reed's hair as he leaned against Keith's chest and moaned. It would be over too soon—he knew that. Reed was too good, tonguing the slit like he was fucking it, caressing his balls, and Keith murmured, "You like this, baby boy," and that was it. He shot down Reed's throat harder than he'd ever remembered coming before. He called out, an indecipherable moan, and then he whimpered like he was some kind of goddamned virgin.

He wasn't sure how long they stayed like that, Reed remaining between his legs, continuing to lick Shane's cock lightly, Keith holding him up, but he wanted it to be for fucking forever, because that's how good it was. For that moment, he was whole and everything was right with the world.

But it wasn't. There was still Guthrie. And Reed was leaving and nothing was secure about his place here. Not yet.

But they were certainly offering to make him some kind of home.

Finally, Reed stood and kissed both Shane and Keith. So goddamned dirty, since they were all tasting Shane's come, and he got hard again.

"He's got to go," Keith told him, and Shane managed to move off of Keith. He watched the men embrace, fought the urge to touch them, instead contented himself with watching, convinced that the two men would start fucking again in front of him.

But judging from what he'd seen and witnessed, they might've actually fucked themselves out. And then Keith walked away, leaving Shane with Reed.

"Like I said, I won't be gone long. Get to know Keith. The job. This place. I think you already like it here. And us."

"Keith's a lot like Kyle," Shane admitted. "Kyle was a hard ass too. Didn't take my shit. I gave him a lot of it in the beginning."

"Been there." Reed smiled as though enjoying the memories. "Am still there sometimes, but I guess I choose to be."

Shane touched his lips self-consciously, thinking about what he'd just done.

And Reed and Keith were going about their business like nothing happened.

Although, that wasn't true, entirely. There was still a raised flush on Reed's face. He'd been affected.

Finally, Reed said, "Keith's like Kyle. You feel like it's a betrayal."

"Keith scares me," he said stubbornly.

"Because you know it can bring you peace."

And peace would be a betrayal. "Where is Kyle's peace?"

"Knowing you're happy," Reed said before he picked up his bag and walked out the door.

It closed with a soft snick of an automatic lock that mimicked the sound of an un-safetied rifle. And now, he was alone. With Keith.

Reed trusted both of them that much. Shane felt humbled and worried all at once as he watched Reed get into a waiting black truck that maneuvered through the snow and ice. Watched for a long time afterwards too, his body still humming with contentment.

He didn't notice Keith come up next to him until the man spoke. "He gets like that when he goes. Cocky as hell."

"And hot," Shane murmured. "And hot," Keith agreed.

"What's he like when he comes back?"

"Stick around and find out."

He planned to. The sky looked ominous and as if to give him fair warning, a few light snowflakes fluttered down.

They were nothing but a preview, according to the weather station Keith watched in the kitchen as he prepared dinner. Shane padded in there, butterflies forming in his stomach, because he had no idea what to expect, what he wanted to expect.

And maybe that was the problem.

"I cook," he announced finally, feeling more than a little idiotic.

Keith handed him a knife, handle first. "Can you do the sides while I season the meat?"

"I can do the whole thing if you want to relax."

"I don't know what that word means," Keith muttered. "Thanks for the offer, though."

They worked in silence for a few moments, until Keith said, "I'm guessing you don't know what the word means either."

"What's that supposed to mean?"

"Exactly what it sounds like."

After a few more minutes of silence and what Shane supposed was a guilty conscience, Shane finally asked, "You want to ask me how I knew about the bridge, don't you?" and Keith shrugged. "Okay, fine. I won't talk about it then. I just know you got pissed at Reed for letting me in on your mission. But he only did when you needed help and I insisted."

Keith didn't say anything or even look up at him and Shane wondered why the hell he was bothering. Instead, he viciously cut the vegetables, wishing he had his old knife that he'd lost somewhere in…

Fuck. He was forgetting where he'd been now. He put the knife down and walked out of the kitchen to catch his breath. The flashback threatened to derail him completely. He felt hot and cold at the same time, his body strung dangerously tight and he swore he heard shots and yells…

"Shane, can you come back to me?" Keith asked, his voice low like he was talking to a dangerous animal.

Which was exactly what Shane could turn into now, he knew. He nodded, managed, "I'm okay," even though he wasn't.

"No, you're not. But that's okay too."

He couldn't have said anything nicer. Shane smiled a little, even though Keith couldn't see it, his body relaxed marginally. He blinked several times, forcing himself to notice the details of the cabin, to ground himself in the here and now instead of traveling back to the past that was following him here, there and every-goddamned-where.

"Come on—I'm starving. You must be too," Keith urged, his voice neutral and after a long moment, he followed Keith back into the kitchen and started putting the cut-up vegetables into the pan for sautéing. Without thinking, Shane cooked them, lost in a semi-daze but pretty confident he wouldn't be slipping into some kind of fugue state. Keith's presence alone seemed to be strong enough to stop that from happening.

When they were ready, he plated them around the grilled meat that Keith finished on the snowy deck off the kitchen. He came in with red cheeks, bringing the crisp air with him.

"Just in time—if we'd waited, I'd never have been able to use the grill."

As he said it, hailstones began to hit the cabin with the familiar tings that Shane had grown used to. Sounded like they could break glass. Keith turned up the TV like he was trying to block the sounds, which were coming like mini-explosions now, and motioned to the table. They ate in relative silence, both half watching the Clint Eastwood western that was coming in with some spotty reception.

When it went out completely, leaving just white snow, Keith reached over and clicked it off. Cleared his throat and said, "I'm trying my best not to scare you. Reed's orders. I guess it's not working."

Shane wasn't sure how to answer that, because most of it wasn't Keith's fault. After careful consideration, he said, "You think I'm trouble."

"I know you're trouble—that's the difference." Keith passed the platter of steak to him and he took it and chewed on Keith's words for a while, along with a second helping of dinner.

Kyle used to tease him like that as well. Shane had a big past to overcome. With Kyle's help, he'd gotten over that. Until Kyle was killed and all the nightmares began again, along with the new one that tailed him from city to city. He'd kept his mouth shut, which made him ashamed, especially because it turned out not to be enough. The man who'd killed Kyle wanted him dead, and he wasn't stopping. And he should've been able to handle that, to get revenge, was angrier at himself than Guthrie even, for being such a fucking coward.

The weather outside wasn't stopping either, which meant that, for now at least, he might be safe. Should be, with the brick wall of man across from him who Shane was pretty sure could fire a gun as easily as breathing. If he was Force Recon, he was also a master at hand-to-hand combats— all types—and some other tricks that Shane had wanted to learn.

Maybe you could tell Keith the whole story, ask him to help you... And maybe you can ice skate in hell too.

"You are way too deep in thought when you're supposed to be eating," Keith said, pulling him from his reverie.

"Yeah," he muttered, and began to eat the hearty meal. Hadn't realized how hungry he actually was until the food began to fill his stomach and he got that warm, pleasant sleepy feeling only a good meal could give you.

"Now you can tell me what you were thinking about," Keith said when they'd both had seconds and Shane picked at thirds with Keith's approval.

"This is the first place I've ever been where I didn't want to leave, to move on to something different or better," he admitted in a rush, the words coming out before he could even give proper thought to them. I belong here would've followed if he hadn't finally been able to censor himself.

As it was, Keith was staring at him. "You haven't been here long enough to know that."

"Bullshit. Reed said he knew after two days. I've been here for what feels like forever."

Keith didn't deny it but then added, "It's been a month and a half, Shane."

"A good month and a half."

"I can't deny that." He paused. "What happened when you were with Kyle? You wanted to move on?"

"I must sound disloyal as hell—I didn't mean that. Kyle and I were great together. But I was always restless on the career front. Wanted to do more, but I had to put in my time. I'm slightly impatient."

"Hadn't noticed," Keith said dryly. "Maybe you're not impatient here because you haven't been here long enough."

"Or maybe it just feels right."

Keith didn't argue with that, looked at Shane with a contented smile on his face. "You know what we do for a living, right?"

"A little bit."

"I can show you more. You can be as involved as you want—or you can help run things from the sidelines."

"You're offering me a job?"

"You can't just sit around and watch movies…and me and Reed."

"That was better than any movie," Shane mumbled before he could help himself, his cock hardening at the mention of it. "Shit. Sorry—things just slip out sometimes."

"You did sleep like a baby last night."

A big aroused one, he wanted to add, but he didn't. Instead, he brought his hands up and massaged his own neck. Lying in a bed for weeks and then pushing it too hard during a workout did not equal happy muscles.

Keith approached him, then ran his big hands across Shane's shoulders. "Relax, boy. I'm just getting some of the tension out. Not going to hurt you."

Had he thought Keith would hurt him physically? "You really don't mind that I kissed Reed when you weren't there?"

"I didn't mind. And I watched today, didn't I? If I minded, don't you think I would've stopped it then and there, not let it continue?" Keith asked. "Look, it's not like we were auditioning for another threesome. It worked with Bobby for a long time. We never planned on inviting someone else into our lives like that, because lightning doesn't strike twice. But obviously, Reed and I are comfortable with the dynamic, enough to give it a try. I don't know how comfortable you are with it. The deeper we get, the more you'll know."

Shane took that in as he put his head down and let Keith's hands work their magic.

Once Keith jumped in to this for real, it would become a fast-moving train, speeding down the tracks and more right than he could possibly imagine. And Shane would find himself dangerously and uncomfortably close to his own truth...would have to decide if he was going to share more or cut and run.

After he'd loosened Shane's muscles, Keith insisted he'd clean up. Directed Shane to Keith and Reed's bedroom and Shane didn't argue, because he didn't want to sleep alone tonight, not with the way the storm raged. He even managed to convince himself that that was the only reason.

"Such bullshit," he muttered to himself as he slid under the covers on Reed's side of the bed. Wanted to crawl into the middle so he'd be sure to be touching Keith but didn't want to push it.

Keith came in about an hour later with his iPad and a laptop. He put them down in the middle of the bed, and Shane noted it was the same tracking system pulled up on the screen that Reed had used the other night.

"Is Reed all right?"

"Other people need to worry about being all right when Reed's on a mission, not the other way around."

Shane believed that Reed could be dangerous, as Keith implied. He didn't know for sure what Reed had been in the Army, beyond medic and then doctor, because Reed hadn't offered the information. Shane's gut leaned toward special forces. Delta made the most sense, because those guys kept their positions classified even after they retired for safety reasons, their own and their family's. "You sure he's okay?"

"He won't even be in country until we wake up," Keith told him. "Then I'll be watching him every second."

Shane nodded, realized his eyes were getting heavy.

"You need to get some sleep if we're going to start some training tomorrow."

The ball of nerves started working his stomach again, even as Keith pulled the covers over him. As Shane drifted off into a much-needed sleep, he realized he'd reached out to grab Keith's hand and held it tight.

In kind, Keith moved closer, put his body against Shane's. "Sorry," he mumbled.

"It's okay, Shane. I don't mind."

Hours later, he woke from a sound sleep at a loud thump outside the house. Before he could figure out where the hell he was or what happened, Keith had pulled him close, murmured, "Just a tree down."

"On the house?"

Keith snorted. "You're safe, PFC," and then in a softer

tone, "You're a good man who's been through hell. Cut yourself some slack."

He wondered if there would ever come a time for him that he would actually be a comfort for Keith. Hadn't realized how badly he wanted that until that moment.

Keith kissed the back of his neck, and Shane shivered. Keith's hand moved down his chest and abs to his cock, the fat head poking up through the waistband of the shorts.

His body went rigid as Keith's hand circled him. A few strokes and Shane moaned. Fuck, it felt better than he could've imagined. Reed and Keith had been the first men to touch him since Kyle, and it felt right that this was happening when Shane was resting on Reed's pillow, inhaling his scent. The tall man was still with them and in that moment, Shane figured he might actually be able to understand how this threesome could work.

Don't think about anything else…all the obstacles on your end, he ordered himself.

"You're thinking way too much," Keith told him, stroked him harder until all Shane could focus on was his cock and Keith's touch, and it was all going to be over too soon.

Shane had been shaking when he woke to the tree falling. Keith had been awake anyway, tracking Reed's progress to the LZ. He was always unable to sleep when Reed was actively working but he knew Shane wouldn't have slept at all without this pretense.

The second he'd gone to comfort him, his body went from zero to sixty, and he knew he wasn't going to be able to roll over and let Shane go back to bed.

Now, listening to the sweet moans the man was making, he knew he'd made the right decision. He sucked then licked the back of Shane's neck and the younger man jumped and said, "Yeah."

Keith thought about asking permission and decided fuck it and moved to flip Shane onto his back. He teased his nipples and he looked up to see Shane's small smile of pleasure even as he protested a little at the bites.

Just you wait, baby boy. Just you wait.

After he crawled down between Shane's legs, he bit the inside of the younger man's thighs lightly and Shane jolted, more in surprise than any pain. He was so fucking sensitive, and Keith was really going to enjoy this. He licked around Shane's balls, coming close but never touching them, and Shane groaned in frustration, went as far as to try to tug Keith's head there.

But Keith refused, instead looked up to see Shane watching him. "Tell me what you want."

"Your mouth, Keith. I want you sucking my cock." Shane reached down to give it a few sharp tugs, and Keith watched him. Thought about ordering Shane to jack himself off while he watched and tucked that away for later.

"You sure? 'Cause I thought I scared you."

Shane was silent for a long moment and then admitted,

"You do."

That made Keith smile, even as his hand trailed down the boy's stomach and landed over Shane's hand, which was still curled around his cock. Shane drew in a sharp breath at the contact, and Keith rubbed hard as Shane pushed back moaning at the friction.

His other hand came up to Keith's head, his touch tender along his shaved scalp, like he was trying to draw the man as close as possible without actually kissing him. Keith moved up finally and did kiss him, hard, fast, loving the way Shane responded.

Their hands moved in tandem, and Shane was moaning—he was at the edge, and Keith pushed him over by telling him, "Come, Shane. And then I'll clean you up with my tongue while you watch."

The thought of that made Shane climax harder than he had in forever. He felt the warm come spurt between them, whispered, "Jesus," with his eyes closed, head against the wall.

And when he felt Keith move away, he looked down to see the big man kneeling between his legs, shaved head bobbing as a rasping tongue cleaned the come off Shane's belly as promised...and finally, rasped over the head of his cock.

"Jesus. Fuck." There was nothing for Shane to do when Keith slid his cock inside his mouth, deep-throated him, and he tried not to come again immediately. Wanted the sensation of being sucked to last for fuckingever…

But he was too far gone for that, even after he'd just come.

"I'm not going to last," he pleaded to Keith, and the man actually smiled around his cock. He bucked his hips up slightly and Keith caught them, pressed them down so he could set the rhythm. Maddeningly slow, and Shane still sensitive and Keith didn't care. Was tonguing the tip of his cock, circling the slit, pressing it until Shane cried out in frustration and pleasure.

He ran his hands along Keith's skull, pulled the man in tighter as Keith opened his throat and took him in, letting Shane fuck his mouth and loving every goddamned minute of it. He gripped Shane's thighs hard, knowing it would leave marks.

He would fuck this baby boy at some point.

Shane whimpered as Keith cupped his balls. He fingered the perineum behind it with a rougher touch, and yeah, baby boy liked that. If he was a sub, Keith would talk about piercing him here, like he'd told Reed he was going to do many a time. Because Reed got turned on by fantasies like that, although in real life, neither was into piercing. But Shane made Keith reconsider all of that.

"Keith, yeah," Shane breathed now as Keith tongued his balls as his hand stroked the thick, hard cock, squeezing drops of precome from the tip. Keith licked that, looked up at Shane to find the boy watching him intently.

So this was how it was going to be. Another Dom, just

like Bobby. And that suited Keith just fine.

He wondered if Reed knew this, but he doubted it. Keith hadn't realized it until Shane's kiss.

Keith moved one of his hands down to Shane's balls again, squeezed them lightly but enough to get the reaction he wanted, which was Shane trying to just not go through the ceiling. He closed his eyes and panted as Keith continued his sweet torture, never letting up until Shane was coming again, this time calling out Keith's name.

Shane wasn't sure when Keith stopped sucking him—all he recalled was the big man wrapping himself around him tightly. Shane was shaking, but this time, there was no fear involved. He was content. Satiated. And, for the moment, calm.

The helo Reed had boarded eventually delivered him to the plane that dropped him in Bogota. Reed had worked that area extensively for the Army, so his familiarity meant he was called often to the location. He didn't pass up the opportunity to look at recent maps and check out new skirmishes in the area—all of it changed the landscapes he was used to and he had to be prepared for any eventuality.

He'd been surprised when he'd learned he'd been culled for that elite Delta Force training. He'd wanted med school, but he'd been convinced that he could accomplish both.

Delta expanded on what he already had—patience, control and speed. He'd worked on strength but he'd also learned many ways to kill a man that required little effort. That's where the medical training really kicked in.

"Proph sends his best," Gary had told him when he boarded. "Couldn't make it this time, but the file's on the seat."

Prophet was hiding something. Correction—Prophet was always hiding something, but this was bigger than most. But he evaded any of Reed's questions by conveniently not being available for a face-to-face meeting before the op. Instead, Reed worked with Mick, who seemed a little wound up himself but was on point once they broke down the door and watched the kidnappers scatter like bugs.

But they'd regrouped, and he and Mick had made quick work of them. In reality, Reed would've liked more of a fight. Had needed more of a fight.

"This went goatfuck in like three seconds," Mick grumbled, but he wasn't unhappy about getting to punch someone either.

According to the files, all Reed and Mick had to do was make the drop, collect the merchandise and move on. In theory.

In reality, the whole thing was a setup, which became evident as more men rushed in behind the ones they'd taken down.

Reed grabbed the arm around his throat, but it was, predictably, like steel.

Instead of fighting it for long, he threw an elbow and broke the man's rib.

A howl and the guy loosened his grip, but not before getting a nice slice in along Reed's forearm. Reed turned and dropped him smoothly with the side of his palm jabbing at the man's throat. Breaking the Y bone wouldn't kill him, but it could disable him with pain and stop him from calling out.

He'd interrogate the second one who came at him from the side. Reed gave a hard shove, a quick kick to the front of the knee and he went down, landing on his elbow, the gun he'd been holding clattering away.

Reed went for it first, shoved it into his pants and stood over the man, his booted foot on his throat. "Who do you work for?"

He eased up on the pressure for a few moments, letting the man collect himself. And then he spat up at Reed, who put his foot back down, blocking his air. "Have it your way. I can do this forever, although it's going to be boring as hell."

In the end, the man had taken an hour to give up the intel. Reed used a pressure point so he went unconscious instead of killing him. His own people would take care of that. And then he and Mick had moved swiftly back into the plane with their cargo that Mick had found under the floorboards.

Being a doctor in this case was handy—get yourself cut, stitch yourself up and move on. Reed did just that, whizzed the needle through the cut on his arm, shot himself up with antibiotics and moved on.

Shane's body was still humming from the blowjob—the most intense one he'd ever received. And then he'd fallen back into a deep sleep, no longer noticing or caring about the wind that seemed like it would whip the house off its foundation.

Now, he heard it still howling outside. The storm was far from over. Keith was checking the laptop next to him, reached a hand out and ruffled his hair.

Shane ducked his head into the pillow. "Morning."

"You had some dream last night," Keith told him.

His stomach tightened and he sat up. "Shit, did I yell and wake you?"

"You woke me, yeah. But it wasn't a nightmare."

"You're sure?"

"I've seen your nightmares."

"Then what the hell was I…oh." Oh was right, because the dream came flashing back to him at top speed. Him. Keith. Him, being fucked by Keith on the kitchen table.

"My name was used several times."

"Not in vain," Shane offered, his face heated. "Now you're shy?"

"Come on. I'm a red-blooded male who needs a good fuck—and soon."

But Keith didn't do any more than ruffle his hair again and get up to head to the shower. Shane lay back against the mattress, frustrated. It was obvious that he'd gotten a reaction out of the man, because that was more than simple morning wood he'd seen rising between the man's legs, tenting the shorts he'd worn to bed. But he was being held at arm's length.

What did you expect—they'd just invite you in to become a threesome and you'd be one big happy family?

Well…yeah. So stupid on him.

Keith took his phone with him when he showered, keeping it close, just in case. But Reed called when he was making breakfast. He could hear the noise of the chopper blades, knew Reed was yelling even though Keith couldn't hear him well. But they were used to these conversations.

"How's he doing?" Reed asked, his first concern for Shane over telling Keith that he was fine.

"He's okay. Coming around."

"I'm fine, Keith. Everything went as expected."

"Which means everything was goatfuck from the first second."

"Pretty much, yes." He heard the laughter in Reed's voice—fuck-ups like that kept him happy. "Business as usual. I'm in one piece. So's Mick."

Keith had watched their movements for most of the night, heard the interrogation through the earbud Reed and Mick had both worn for this job. This ring of dealers had been on their radars for some time—they were responsible for nearly killing several young men while using an experimental drug, and Prophet's boss had been tasked with taking them down. Mick was running point on the mission, but bringing Reed in first for the initial sweep was a bigger part of the plan. After that, Mick would reveal himself to them as a dirty fed who would get the group what they needed to continue with their illegal enterprises.

They'd run scams like this before on criminals, but it was always risky.

"Come home," he told Reed now. "Can't wait, love."

Keith smiled into the phone. Reed wasn't always affectionate, but the times that he was, even with a single word, he warmed Keith to his damned soul. "We'll be waiting."

"I like the sound of we," Reed said. "He makes you happy. Make him stay."

Keith paused for a long second, considering the he-makes-you-happy part and still refusing to admit it, and then said, "For you."

"For all of us," Reed said simply before he cut the line.

Keith wouldn't do anything until he'd watched Reed get onto the helo and got the call saying everything was good.

"Another successful mission," Shane said.

"Now we train," Keith told him, brushing past him and forcing Shane to follow into the padded room.

"Did you add this on?"

"No, this was here."

"Looks like a big dining room or something." He pointed to the ceiling pattern. "Are you sure this place wasn't ever an inn?"

"Not that I was ever able to find out—and I tried," Keith told him. "Are you stalling?"

He was, knew he'd have to fake it a little during this,

for self-preservation. He knew Keith would be looking for signs of what he could do…but he was still weak enough that he honestly didn't have to work very hard on evasion at all.

"Yeah, I'm stalling." Shane rolled his eyes.

"Might want to lose the attitude," Keith said casually after he'd flipped Shane onto his back and held him there with a foot on his chest. Shane was breathing—wheezing more accurately—like an eighty-year-old smoker. Everything felt tight, his muscles ached simultaneously from both over- and underuse. But at least his ribs were wrapped tightly enough that they were protected.

They were nearly healed anyway.

"So you and Reed would really consider giving me a job?" Shane asked from his position on the floor.

"Don't you need one?"

"I need to deal with Guthrie first." And then the CIA would clear him. And then…

"I know you need to take care of Guthrie. But that can't be your whole life.

Kyle wouldn't want that."

Shane wanted to be angry with Keith for bringing up Kyle's name so freely but in truth he was sick of being angry. Keith and Reed made him feel something other than that emotion.

"Work first, talk later." Keith asked him more about his training, and Shane lied and said that Kyle had taught him a great deal. "Good, show me."

Keith looked like a serious brick wall. Kyle told him men like that went down hard, but after Shane tried a few moves on him, it was apparent that didn't hold true in all situations. And Shane had to hold back. As an operative, he learned a lot of different fighting methods, including the ways a Force Recon Marine would've trained. But he'd be giving himself away if he made any moves that belied anything beyond Army Ranger.

He was out of shape as well, which would help with the ruse.

"You didn't do badly," Keith told him later. Shane didn't have the strength to speak, just gave Keith the middle-finger salute.

"Hey, I expected you to be in way worse condition," Keith offered. A rare, if not grudging compliment.

He and Keith lay on their backs on the mat, sweaty, tired and flying, much like they'd be after sex. And God, it would be so easy to roll over onto Keith right now and ask for what he wanted.

Too easy. And he never took easy.

He couldn't remember why, though. Maybe there had never been an explanation. And so to distract himself, he said, "It must be hard for you to let Reed go on jobs without you."

"Is that the same thing you asked him while I was gone?"

"Yes."

Keith laughed a little. "He and I are good together on missions, but we're also a liability to one another. It's too personal. And it took us a long time to recognize that."

"I can see that. You know, Reed doesn't look like an operative at first glance. He should, because once you see him move, you know, but…" Shane couldn't explain it, but Keith nodded.

"That's the thing with Reed. They don't see him coming."

"I would," Shane said.

"But you were trained to spot predators." Shane considered the truth in that.

"Were you courted for Delta?"

"No." That was the truth. "What about Kyle?"

"He liked being a Ranger, but he knew being asked for Delta was major. He just wanted to be the best at what he was, you know? Always training, looking to learn more from everyone. He was the least cocky guy I knew…and somehow, that made him the most cocky."

Keith grinned like he knew the type. Because he was the damned type, but Shane wouldn't give him the satisfaction of telling him that.

"What are you thinking about?" Keith asked, rolling onto his side to stare down at Shane.

"Suppose it doesn't work out?"

"Which part, Shane?"

"Both. Or suppose just the job works but the other…"

"Then you could still work for us—with us—and live

someplace else. It's not an all-inclusive deal. And you might decide you don't want the job."

But Shane did. One look at the kinds of things they did and he knew he was all in. They helped people in need and apparently, it wasn't all about the money. The clients they took, many of them, couldn't afford to pay.

He hoped he could also be one of the success stories. He liked the fact that they didn't expect him to sit back and do nothing. And after he showered, he made up a file on Guthrie, culling everything he could from memory and listing it all in one place. Making his case, figuring ways to catch him.

It felt good to do something besides run and hate.

Kyle might want him to find peace, but he'd also know Shane wouldn't have let his good name go unavenged.

"You smile when you think about him, you know," Keith said. "It's a good sign."

"You think?"

"Took me months before I could think about Bobby and be happy at all. But then I started thinking about how we first got together—how he was frustrating as hell and what a pain in the ass I was to him because of it…"

He shook his head at the memory, and Shane understood what he meant. Kyle had been equally frustrating in the beginning as well. He'd had to chase the man carefully, as he'd been an officer and Shane was a private and it was all so inappropriate. Which made Kyle's surrender—when he'd finally given in—that much more satisfying.

He told all that to Keith, who said, "So what finally happened?"

"After that barfight and the kiss I told you about— he practically shoved me into my car and for weeks we pretended it didn't happen. But one night, I just showed up at his place, finally knocked on his door and didn't give him a chance to say no."

"You took a big risk."

Not really, since he wasn't exactly Army, but Kyle could've reported him anyway. But he hadn't. Instead, the man kissed him back and Shane dragged him to the couch, bent him over and fucked him until he was barely coherent. And then he'd taken him to the bedroom and fucked him more.

From the first time he'd talked to the man, he'd been pretty sure he'd been in love with him. By the end of their first weekend together, he knew he was.

Keith studied him for a while and then said, "Why don't you tell me everything you know about Guthrie. I don't want to do a search on him and raise any flags. And he sounds like he's good."

Shit. Shane should've anticipated this. Keith was alternately relaxing him and then pumping him for intel— and it should've been intel that Shane could easily talk about. Instead, he'd need to proceed very carefully, trying to remember the lies and half-truths he'd been taught about

Guthrie, the CIA agent he was working undercover with.

"He is. He was a Ranger for twenty years. Took early retirement."

"You're sure?"

"Of what?"

"That he was only a Ranger?"

Shane should know better about trying to fool Keith. "As far as I knew, yes." Keith seemed satisfied with that.

"I didn't know much about him—he was in Kyle's company, not mine."

"How old would he be?"

"Maybe forty?" he guessed. But in reality, he knew the man was forty-two, knew his birthdate, his address, his bank account number. He knew more about Guthrie than Guthrie did.

Then why are you still running?

That was the one question he still wasn't able to answer.

15

Shane heard the bathroom door open and pretended not to. The glass in the sauna shower was clear, and although they were steamed up, he was pretty sure Keith could see most of him.

He figured he came in for a towel. After last night and the blowjob, the reference to Shane's dream, Keith acted like he was nothing more than a friend and now, especially after the sparring and talk of first times with Kyle, Shane was hard and more frustrated than he'd been in a long time.

Maybe last night was something Keith regretted, although he didn't seem like a man who lived with regrets or did things he regretted in the first place.

He'd been so deep inside his own head that he hadn't heard the shower door open or close, but then Keith was at his back under the spray. Shane tensed at first, because his scars were on full display, especially when Keith circled his wrists with his hands and pushed them forward.

"Hold the tile," he told Shane who wanted to buck at the commands. He was the one who would normally be giving them, but his body seemed to melt and follow whenever Keith spoke.

Keith ran his hands along Shane's arms. "You're going to be sore tomorrow."

Shane didn't know if he was talking about the workout—or referencing what would happen now. And what was worse, he was praying it was the latter.

He hadn't thought about the dynamics of being alone with one man or the other. How did that work?

He guessed he was about to find out, but if you'd asked him a week ago, he would've guessed he and Reed would've been together first. Keith intimidated him, for some reasons he'd figured out and others he hadn't.

But oh, how he wanted—wanted to be taken by this man. He rarely bottomed, never gave much thought as to why, since when it was the right top, it was goddamned motherfucking awesome.

"What did I do to you in your dream?" Keith asked. He closed his eyes, his cheeks heating. "You...I..."

"Relax, Shane." Keith kissed the back of his neck, rubbed his back until Shane was able to start over.

"I was mouthing off to you at the table."

"Dreams imitating life," Keith murmured.

"And then you grabbed me and pushed me down. And you fucked me over the table. And I loved it."

His voice was hoarse on the last words. Broke a little too, which he didn't understand. Keith sucked the back of his neck and then turned the shower off, dried them both. And then walked them out to the kitchen, as Shane suspected.

He whimpered a little when they got close to the table and Keith brushed a palm over the smooth surface, as if readying it for him. And then he pointed for Shane to bend over it and Shane knew he'd blush every goddamned time he sat here from now on.

"I can't."

"Why?"

"I don't bottom."

"Ever?"

"Not for a long time, Keith."

"But for me, you want to."

Shane opened his mouth and then closed it, because Keith spoke a truth he hadn't been able to see, even though it had been right in front of his face.

But then Keith touched his ribs. "We'll save this for later."

"I don't want to save anything."

"I'm still fucking you, Shane—just not on this surface." His hand brushed Shane's still-healing ribs and Shane shivered at the warmth, especially when Keith's arm wrapped around his waist and led him back toward Shane's bedroom. Gave him a slight push onto the bed.

Shane gathered the pillow under his head, his hands fisted into its underside as he lay there, vulnerable. He tensed as Keith's tongue ran along his lower back, but Keith either didn't notice or didn't care. Figured it was the latter and willed himself not to pull back.

Excitement and nerves bundles together in his gut as he pushed onto his hands and knees, spread his legs, opening himself to Keith. An offering, something he didn't do easily.

Keith licked along the crease of his thigh, his ass. He heard himself suck in a harsh breath and then released it with a huff. His entire body simultaneously tightened and subsequently relaxed as the pleasure jolted through him.

He couldn't remember the last time he'd been rimmed. Couldn't understand why he'd waited this long.

He was rocking into Keith's tongue, lowered himself to his elbows, forehead pressed to the mattress. Incoherence took over his brain, his body moved on its own accord, wanting Keith to take him over. Needing him to. This surrender was so personal, and Keith knew it.

All Shane needed to do was accept it and so he did. Keith's tongue probed the most sensitive, intimate place Shane could imagine. Prone, spread, trembling.

He heard a moan push past his lips as his balls tightened. He felt the precome leak from his cock, knew that he could come easily with just a few tugs.

But Shane had never done things the easy way, so he figured, why start now?

"If you're thinking, I'm doing something wrong," Keith whispered.

"You're doing everything right," he told the man who slid his body on top of his.

Shane pushed back impatiently, but the big man wouldn't be rushed, instead ghosted his lips across the back of Shane's neck, then his shoulders, marking him in far subtler and more effective ways than Shane had him.

He groaned with impatience, his body fighting against the shuddering and ultimately losing.

"That's it, baby boy. No shame in giving in," Keith told him, his voice soothing, his hands making everything okay. His cock pressed against Shane's ass, and he willed himself not to tense up again. He remained like that for long moments, his mind going a hundred miles an hour, and he wanted Keith to go and stop and everything in between.

Keith moved away, his hand resting on Shane's lower back, pressing him down, holding him there. Grounding him. His breathing eased but his hands were numb from fisting them so hard.

Keith's finger circled his hole, the warm lube tingling as the finger entered him. He bit back a groan until Keith told him harshly, "I want to goddamned hear your pleasure."

Two fingers, twisted and Shane couldn't have held back if he'd wanted to. "Keith!"

"Yeah, that's it. Who owns you, baby boy?"

Christ. He almost came there and then. Forced himself not to because he knew there would be so much more pleasure if he waited. But that didn't stop him from whimpering like a fucking baby the second Keith spoke the words.

"I knew you liked that. But what do you like more—being called baby boy or being owned?"

"Both," he said before he could stop himself, and then he groaned again, because Keith's knuckle was brushing his prostate and the mind-bending pleasure speared through him.

When the fingers came out, he knew what would replace them. Felt Keith's cock probe his ass, and he tensed but Keith was gentle, moved slowly. Babied the fuck out of him, which, for some strange reason, he resented.

But you don't mind being called baby boy.

Shane didn't appear to need seduction, although it appeared that his entire stay had been one long seduction.

Keith settled comfortably between his legs. The man under him was holding back, afraid of hurting Keith, maybe, which was understandable. Men like him weren't used to be around others who could give as good as they got. Which meant his story about Kyle training him had been utter and complete bullshit. Shane was coiled tight, unwilling to move for fear of bucking Keith off.

"You can move, Shane. Come on," he urged, but all Shane did was push himself back to his knees and elbows. It was the best position, given the rib fractures, but Keith wanted him on his back, wanted to watch his face when he came.

Beggars couldn't be choosers though, and he wasn't

giving up any opportunity with this naked man.

"Come on, old man—what's the holdup?" Shane asked and grunted when Keith pushed his cock halfway inside the tight channel, holding one of Shane's hips, the other on the man's shoulder to gain further purchase.

Shane pushed back against him. Groaned when Keith met the thrust and slid in balls-deep and immediately started to pump his hips, because it felt that good. Shane agreed, if the way his hands gripped the sheets was any indication.

There were no protests from his mouth, just fuck and more and Keith's name, and Keith did fuck him more, harder, the bed rattling under them, pillows falling, pictures on the wall above the bed threatening to join them, reminding Keith why he and Reed and Bobby never fucked in this room.

He pulled Shane's back up against his chest, not wanting the man to get beaned in the head from falling frames, took advantage of him by holding both hips firm and pistoning against him. Shane was jacking himself off, and he was so close, if the sounds he made were any indication.

Just because Shane resented the tenderness didn't mean he didn't fucking love it when Keith worked his cock inside of him, until Keith's balls slapped his ass on the final push.

And then Keith was fucking him, the gentleness gone,

the mattress moving under the weight of both men and finally—finally—his goddamned mind quieted and all that was left was Keith's cock inside ofhim.

"Who owns you, baby boy?" Keith asked again, and Shane whispered, "You do. You both do."

Keith's hand rewarded him with a sharp slap to his ass, followed immediately by a soothing rub. "That's the way you want it."

"How do you want it?" Shane couldn't help but ask. "Just the way you said."

Shane moaned at his words, thinking maybe, just maybe, it could all work and holy hell, Keith was fucking him in earnest now, pistoning his hips, taking Shane so fast it was a constant assault on his prostate, and it had never been this good getting fucked.

But the best part was, he was getting Shane ready to be fucked by Reed. And it might not happen tonight or this week, but Keith was breaking him in. Getting him ready.

He could handle it. But the thing was, he didn't know if he wanted to. Because a part of him ached to bend Keith over and give as good as he'd gotten.

"Come for me, baby boy," Keith growled, and Shane dropped his head back with a groan of surrender. He'd been forced to go to a place he'd never known existed.

How long had he been fooling himself?

There were cigarette burns on Shane's body. Keith recognized them immediately, because he'd seen enough kids wearing the same scars that lasted a lifetime.

"He only got me once," Shane said. Keith hadn't realized he'd been running his finger across the twin marks as they lay on the rug in front of the fire where Keith had led him after they'd fucked their brains out—literally, it seemed at some point—on the table. "The next time he tried, I was ready. Slammed his hand with a baseball bat and broke his wrist."

"Bet you didn't stay there long."

Shane looked at him with a hint of guilt for the early lie he'd told about his parents. "I wasn't going to, anyway. None of those places are ever permanent and everyone knows it. They just tell you to be good because that'll get you adopted so they don't have to find you a new home after you fuck up and get kicked out." Shane's chin jutted, but Keith saw the boy behind the man at that moment. The pain reflected there, but hell, that's what made him who he was.

"I get that."

"Do you?"

"More than you realize," Keith said, but Shane left it at that. Probably because he didn't want to discuss it further himself. Most walks down memory lane ended badly.

But tonight hadn't. It felt so damned right. Despite

Keith's suspicions, despite everything, tonight with Shane had pushed the walls he'd tried to hold up more than three quarters of the way down.

Shane's hand moved to tweak Keith's nipple. "That all you got?" Keith asked.

"No, I have a lot more." He looked up at Keith. "When I was sixteen, I started sneaking into a club about an hour from where I lived. In the big city. They took pity on me—a kid from the sticks who knew he was gay and knew he liked to dominate. Who the hell else was gong to help me, you know?" He smiled at the memory. "The guy who owned and ran the place was named Chief. A big bear of a leather daddy. He was a good mentor. Most of the time, I was scared to death. I'm sure they all saw it, but they were surprisingly kind. Maybe I reminded them of them, you know?"

"You probably did," Keith told him.

"They didn't touch me until I turned eighteen. I just got to watch and listen. It was like, porn, up close and personal." But it had been more than that, because for sure, he watched relationships grow between men. Learned that emotions grew through sex and that it was okay to want to tie men up and fuck them. That it didn't make him sick or twisted… and that it did make him twisted in a good way. "I tried everything. Top, bottom and every flavor in between. I was like a sponge, wanted to soak it all up," Shane admitted.

"I can see that now," Keith told him. "It's always the quiet ones you have to watch out for."

And that was true—Shane had been quiet. Focused. He knew what he wanted. Knew he was going into a program that was notoriously homophobic— although once inside, he realized those claims were really unjustified in most cases. He just didn't talk about his personal life in terms of male or female, and no one pushed or made a big deal out of anything.

But in the back rooms of that club, he'd let himself be tied down, spanked and whipped, and he'd done things that pushed him uncomfortably beyond his limits. But at least he'd learned what those were, Chief told him. Safe, sane, consensual became the most important words in his vocabulary, and with the help of several Doms he also realized that, while he did like the top and certain aspects of domination, he wasn't looking for any kind of full-time gig.

But the dominant part of him, well, there was no controlling that. For him, the best part of sex was watching his partner give their submission—it was a goddamned gift. And all he wanted to do was bring pleasure to whoever gave him that gift.

Keith was watching him with that look somewhere between serious and amused when he talked about the clubs and the other stuff. "Bobby spent time in the leather clubs back in the day. Once we got together, not so much. We couldn't risk it, and then, once we could, we were here and happy. And then Reed came along."

"So, ah, you and Bobby and Reed worked because of your preferences?"

Keith gave him a small smile. "Nothing in the sexual arena's that black or white—shouldn't be, anyway, but yeah, I guess that's a good way to put it. It's not like we grew up looking for a threesome, but when we found it, we just knew it was right."

"So Reed…he probably wouldn't be comfortable with me, then?"

"Why not?"

"Because that's not the dynamic you had before."

"I'd say it was pretty damned close," Keith said and then everything clicked and the world opened up to Shane. "We all switched it up when we needed to, but for the most part, yeah."

"But what about when it was just you and Bobby?"

"We made it work. You get something different out of each experience. Something imperative. And it helps Reed. Besides, you can't be a good top until you'd spent some time on the bottom."

That was true. Maybe Shane needed to spend more time there, for Reed's sake. And Keith's as well.

16

Reed had been fine on the phone, but there had been enough of a hint in his tone to let Keith know what he'd be dealing with when he returned. Reed was holding it together, and he'd need to lose it when he came back to Keith. It wasn't anything new, and the familiarity itself was almost as much of a comfort to Keith as seeing his lover walk through the door was.

He led the man into their bedroom quietly. Sat him on the edge of the bed, took his bag away and locked it upstairs. Stripped him down halfway and then began to wipe the paint off Reed's face, watching his lover slowly come back to him as he did. This uncovering was part of the ritual for both of them. Reed once said that he couldn't bear to wipe it off himself—that he could do it only through Keith's eyes at first.

And so Keith indulged him. But this time, something was different. Proph said the job was done well, even in the face of unexpected ambush. Neither surprised Keith— Reed was as good at his job if not better than when he was official Delta and ambushes were more expected than not.

Still, Reed was on guard. His muscles tensed when they should've begun to relax. Something had triggered an old reaction in his lover.

"Talk to me, baby," he crooned, and a muscle in Reed's jaw twitched, but he didn't say a word. "Come back to me. I need you."

With that, something changed in Reed's breathing pattern. His eyes blinked like he was waking up from a long dream. "That's it. You're good, baby."

"You've got me," Reed whispered. "I know."

"Welcome home, soldier. How about a hot bath."

Reed nodded. "Gonna shut my eyes for a few minutes while you run the water."

Keith wanted to tell him not to do that, probably should've picked him up and fucked him, anything to keep him awake. But he didn't, because Reed looked so trusting and he didn't want to take away the man's faith in himself. He went into the bathroom and ran the tub, giving Reed some time to fall into the deep sleep he needed.

He shut the water off and waited, listening to the silence, Reed's deep breathing and he convinced himself that everything would be okay.

He was proven wrong within the next fifteen seconds.

Shane heard the screams and at first, thought it was him.

He'd fallen asleep on the couch watching a movie and when he looked at the door, he noted that Reed's boots and bag were there.

Reed was screaming. Was he hurt? Why hadn't Keith woken him up?

He covered the area between the living room and bedroom in seconds, found Keith trying to hold a struggling Reed down on the bed.

There was no blood and he didn't appear to be injured.

"What can I do?" he asked, and Keith turned, his expression unreadable. "Just help me hold him down and be careful. He's strong coming out of these dreams."

Shane moved fast, helped Keith immobilize the struggling man. Reed was flailing, scratching and clawing and bucking every touch and what the hell had happened to make him dream like this? Finally, he let Keith deal with his upper body and he managed to immobilize the man's legs, at least long enough for Keith to inject him with something.

Within five minutes, Reed's fighting was less. Although he didn't pass out completely, he seemed to almost come to and realize where he was. Said, "Ah, fuck," a few times and closed his eyes, putting his forearm over them like he didn't want to deal with any of it.

"I only sedate him if things get really bad," Keith said as he motioned for Shane to let go of Reed's legs. He did and Reed's arm moved away from his eyes, resting on his forehead as he seemed to surrender himself to the drug. "It's short-acting. He'll wake up quickly. But he'll hurt himself if I let him stay in the nightmare."

Shane could only imagine. "How often does that happen?"

"Couple times a year. Over the past several weeks, it's been worse." The math was easy enough to do…all since Shane had been there. "Not your fault," Keith said.

"But it's happening because of me, still." Shane reached out and stroked some hair from Reed's face without thinking. The man opened his eyes—hazy from the drugs—and he gripped Shane's wrist.

A grip of goddamned steel. Shane had always known that being in the house with both these man was anything but safe. Maybe that's why his cock hardened with the touch.

"Hey Reed," he said, keeping his voice quiet. Reed gave him a drugged smile, pulled his arm close and kissed the inside of his wrist a couple of times. But the death grip never released.

Keith was watching them intently. "Does this happen?"

"Never."

Shane met Keith's gaze. There was no anger there. Lust, mixed with some emotion just out of reach…

"Shane." Reed's voice.

"Don't underestimate him," Keith warned.

"Reed, you're okay. Tell me what you need." Shane spoke softly. But Reed just grinned like the cat that ate the canary and fell back to sleep. The grip on Shane's wrist loosened a little, but he didn't want to risk waking the man up by pulling away, so he didn't.

There were still traces of camo paint along the sides of Reed's face, even after Keith had painstakingly wiped him down. Shane could see the evidence of that on the washcloths in the basin by the bed. Reed smelled like fresh air. Gun oil. Battle.

"He came in and went to sleep for a few minutes while I was getting the steam shower ready for him. I came back to this," Keith explained.

"Did something happen?"

"If something doesn't happen, the job's not considered a success," Keith said. "But what's happening has nothing to do with this trip."

"He looks almost peaceful," Shane said and Keith barely got out the words, "Don't let that fool you," when Reed lunged up from the bed, grabbed Shane and flipped him onto the floor in one swift, silent and deadly movement.

It was similar to the move Keith had taught him, done with precision and impeccable timing. And it took his breath away, literally. He gasped for air and Keith warned, "Reed, go easy on him."

Reed seemed to come to. Froze. But didn't move off him, kept Shane trapped with his body weight. Shane felt his cock harden. Reed's had already been but Shane thought it might've been in reaction to the fighting. And even though he knew Reed typically relished a more submissive role, Shane knew that wouldn't fly tonight, knew he had to give him the green light to do what he needed to.

"Don't you dare go easy on me," he demanded. "I don't want either of you to go easy on me. I want it rough. I want to feel it for a goddamned week."

Reed didn't need to be told twice, bent his head, kissed Shane, and Shane knew for sure Reed's reaction to grab him was a symptom of something more than wanting sex. Unexpected in this context, but not wholly surprising, all things considered.

It was a fierce kiss, as if Reed had just gotten home from battle and had war beating to the rhythm of his heart. Shane closed his eyes and let Reed melt against him, especially because Keith ran his hands through both men's hair, reassuring. Like he was letting them know he was their safety net. Their anchor.

Shane hadn't realized that he'd ached for this. The touch, the contact. The fucking heat.

He bucked his pelvis against Reed, couldn't help it. His cock needed the friction, and Reed rubbed right back against it, moaning into Shane's mouth.

Reed shoved Shane's pants down to his knees. Keith must've been helping because suddenly it was bare cock against bare cock. He groaned helplessly into Reed's mouth.

"Make him come," Keith ordered Reed, who quickly captured their cocks together in his hand and began to stroke them. It made Shane's balls tighten, his body stiffen faster than he'd thought possible.

"Just like that first night," Reed told him. "You did this to yourself while we watched. Wanted to touch you...but I didn't. Couldn't. Now I can."

"Please..." Shane didn't know what he was asking for but the climax bolted through him before he could say anything more. He whimpered as the force of it drained his cock in several long, satisfying spurts of come that spattered his chest and Reed's.

He buried his face against Reed's neck and breathed the man in as he recovered. When he finally pulled back, Reed was watching him with a slight grin, and yes, he looked much better than he had earlier. Keith wound a hand in the back of his head again and guided him down between Shane's legs again.

"Clean him up," Keith ordered, held Reed's hair, moving his head down as he licked Shane's chest and stomach, cock and balls clean.

"Jesus, I could come again just watching this," Shane breathed. Reed's tongue rasped over his belly and thighs, balls and cock until he was hard and squirming under the ministrations.

"That can be arranged," Keith told him.

"More," he heard himself insist, and Reed smiled, looked up at him even as he took Shane's cock into his mouth, and just the sight of the man's lips stretched around his cock nearly made him come immediately.

But he wanted to have some self-control. Wanted this to last, in case it was a one-and-only scenario, needed it to play out in his fantasies over and over. And so he watched Reed suck him, felt the man's tongue in his slit, hands on his balls…fingers digging into his hips.

"Fuck his mouth," Keith told Shane, and Shane shuddered and rocked his hips against Reed's hot, wet grip. "That's it. Harder. He likes it."

Judging by the happy humming, Reed absolutely did. Keith's hand was on Reed's hair, twined in it, and he reached out to tweak one of Shane's nipples. Hard.

"Fuck." He jumped, and Reed sucked harder as the pain turned to a pleasurable zing that went from abused nipple to groin. Keith did it again and again, and Shane was helpless against Keith's touches…and Keith knew it. Chuckled and leaned forward over Reed's head to suck a nipple into his mouth between his teeth. He teased it with his tongue as Reed turned up the volume on the sucking and humming and the alternating soft and hard wet bites were making Shane threaten to float away.

And he never wanted to come down. With Keith licking his nipples, Shane shot down Reed's throat, and as his cock was milked, he didn't remember much else when he came to on his back on the mattress. His nipples were still wet and his cock sensitive as hell but still half hard.

Two orgasms in the space of no more than twenty

minutes—he hadn't been able to do that since he was seventeen. Maybe Keith was feeding him some kind of aphrodisiac.

Or maybe he was just with the right men.

"Now it's your turn," Keith told him, and he was guiding Shane's head to Reed's thighs. "That's it baby boy, lick him clean."

He shuddered when Keith called him baby boy. Of course, the man noticed immediately, let out a soft chuckle.

What else would Keith make him do? Would he find himself asking for things he wanted Keith to do?

You already did. And it felt right.

Keith pulled him up to a tall kneeling position, gazed down at him unhurriedly and then over to Reed, who lay wantonly in front of them on the floor, legs spread, cock half hard and still big enough to make Shane sweat.

"How can I put the two of you to the best possible use?" Keith pondered out loud. "You Army boys always need a Marine to keep you in line."

Reed laughed at that, and Shane marveled at the deep, rich sounds that came from a man who was in the throes of a horrible nightmare not half an hour earlier. He wanted to pull Reed close and stroke his hair, tell him that he would help to take care of him. Wanted to.

As if they knew what Shane was thinking, both men turned to look at him. This was make or break, and Shane could walk away, not join in and neither man would hold it against him. Keith told him as much.

But he wanted. Goddamned how he wanted more of this, of both of them.

Keith couldn't think of anything more perfect than having these two men at his cock. He ran his hands through their hair as they alternated licking his balls, stroking his shaft, fingering along his perineum until he groaned, threw his head back and fought the inevitable. Every once in a while, their mouths would meet and they would kiss, cheeks pressed to his cock and goddamn, he wished his cock could be in several places at once, filling both men in every possible way.

And then Reed guided Shane's mouth over Keith's cock, held the back of the boy's neck while Keith shot down his throat. Shane took him all in, hummed, and the vibrations made his cock spurt several times longer than he'd expected, especially because Reed was sucking his balls.

Neither man stopped, and Keith wondered how fast he could come again—and as much as he loved being in Shane's mouth, there were other things he planned on doing tonight. He eased Shane away and the younger man smiled up at him, his lips swollen, his eyes heavy-lidded with lust.

He nodded at him, cut his glance to Reed, and Shane's lazy smile got more intense. He watched the two men crawling on each other, first Reed on Shane, until the younger boy hooked his leg around Reed's and flipped him so he landed on top.

Keith pushed up on his elbows, wondering if Reed was surprised by the sudden revelation. If Reed had already known it, he hadn't said.

Shane wasn't submissive, not in the way Reed was. No, Shane was, for all intents and purposes, as much of a top as Keith, as Bobby had been. It was in the way he mastered Reed in that instant, stroking him while holding him down, kissing him into submission so he could have his way with the soldier.

And Keith was going to love watching every minute of it.

He couldn't have handled this position an hour ago, but now, Reed could think of nothing better than Shane's weight on him, holding him, centering him. Shane caught a wrist in his hand and held it above Reed's head, but he left the other free. He ran his hand through the young man's hair, feeling the silkiness between his fingers, watching Keith over Shane's head as he sucked a nipple hard enough to create a jolt of pure pleasure through him.

Shane was hard again—a feat in and of itself, but it was his fingers that probed Reed, first one and then quickly moved up to two and then three. It was a burn of pleasure and pain, a finger over Reed's prostate gave a hot throb to his cock.

"Spread your legs more," Shane said, an order rather than a request, and Reed did so willingly, so fucking turned on by Shane ordering him and Keith watching, ready to give orders if necessary. Both of them, making him submit.

Both of them knowing this was more about making Reed submit to what he wanted than submitting to either man. His breath hitched thinking about it, and Shane smiled down at him as he worked his fingers in and out, and Reed met him stroke for stroke, his cock dripping onto his stomach. He reached down between them to grab for it but Shane swatted his hand away.

"I'll tie you down if I have to," he said, and Keith nodded in agreement, and holy hell, this was quickly becoming unbearable. Shane sucked a nipple and Reed groaned, stared over his head at Keith, who was rubbing Shane's back.

"Fuck him, Shane," Keith said softly. Reed uttered a surprised huff and watched Shane.

"Just do it," Reed growled, which made Shane go even slower. Torturing him as his hole stretched, his body held taut as Shane twisted two fingers inside of him.

"You're not in charge of this one, son," Shane told him, and Reed's mouth opened. His entire body heated and he almost struggled. But, as if Shane knew, everything about Shane changed from the angry man he'd been just a little earlier to comforting and in charge.

He put a hand on the back of Reed's neck. Put his face down so they were forehead to forehead, murmured against Reed's lips, "Just breathe, Reed. Just breathe and stay with me."

Reed did as Shane asked.

His thighs opened, and Shane pressed inside him. The pain and pleasure happened together, wrapped up in a hot rush as Shane's cock filled him, even as he held Reed's wrists to the floor above his head. His hips rocked, and Reed wrapped his legs around Shane's waist in order to drive him in faster. He half expected Shane—or Keith—to stop him from doing so but neither man was in any position to give orders. They were all caught up in the moment, Keith stroking himself, Shane's cock hitting Reed's gland, and Reed came first, crying out hoarsely, even as Shane buried his face in Reed's neck and held him in place until he came as well.

Finally, he released Reed's wrists and Reed brought his hands around Shane's back, dropped his legs away, and finally, he was officially back home.

17

Reed went to sleep, his breaths easy, especially because he was half wound around both men, in the middle of the bed. Keith and Shane both propped on their elbows and pillows, neither man remotely ready for sleep.

Besides, Shane had a feeling that Keith wanted to stay up anyway and make sure Reed was past the point of having flashbacks, for tonight at least. And although he wanted to ask about them, he wasn't sure if he was ready to know why. He still had his own to deal with. Maybe he was shouldering too much.

But he had noted something else...on Keith's inner thigh. Cigarette burns that matched Shane's, and he thought about how quickly he'd dismissed Keith's understanding the night the man had seen Shane's. In actuality, he'd been freaked that Keith might think everything he'd told them was a lie, but so far, Shane got the sense that Keith wanted to believe him, so he did.

Push it all down for now, Shane, he told himself. No good could come of the truth.

"He seems content," Shane said finally, breaking the easy silence, and Keith smiled, especially as Reed curled and nuzzled against his chest. "He needed this. You."

"Reed thinks that he needs me way more than I need him. He doesn't realize how badly I needed him too. Always," Keith said quietly, and Shane waited patiently, which was something he figured Reed never really did.

Keith seemed to appreciate it. "I loved Bobby. We had a certain kind of relationship. We didn't have to talk about the foster-home shit because we both lived it. Or at least, I thought we didn't have to. But my experience and Bobby's were pretty far apart."

"I saw your burns too."

"I figured." Shane put a flat palm on Keith's chest and Keith put a hand over it. "It was a long time ago. I don't have nightmares about it, but it surfaces for me sometimes."

"And you told Reed about it."

"Not at first, but once I realized that his assholeishness was all smoke and mirrors, I did. He was so ashamed that he was having the flashbacks and the nightmares. He felt weak—and men like him don't do well feeling that way, you know? He can take on the world as a soldier, save people as a doctor, but inside…" Keith trailed off, and Shane recalled Reed's terror.

Reed, who now slept like a baby next to them. Shane marveled how open these men were. Amazing really, that Keith could tell Shane this when he couldn't be sure if Reed was hearing it.

He wanted to stay a part of these men so badly it hurt. But for now, he concentrated on Keith and his story, because he wanted to know every last thing about them, for better or for worse.

"It's not like Bobby wouldn't have been sympathetic. I just didn't like worrying him about anything. And I'd pushed it down for forever anyway. But when Reed started to struggle, it all came to the forefront for me."

There was pain etched on Keith's face. He was struggling with it, whether to air it out in the open or keep it buried. At this point, it appeared there were few secrets between the men, any and all boundaries breaking down quickly, thanks to proximity and growing feelings.

When you love someone, it's impossible to hide anything from them for very long, Kyle used to say. Apparently, Keith felt that Shane would figure it out sooner rather than later.

Keith felt himself hesitate, but knew this could be the best thing for all of them. They obviously had chemistry, and it seemed like they had even more. It was time to put up or shut up. "I don't remember my mother. According to what I pieced together, she was young—too young—and she dropped me off at a convent when I was a couple of years old. I didn't know my own name, never mind my birthday, so they kind of estimated. Got me cleaned up, checked out—I was pretty dehydrated. Underweight. Sick. But I was young enough that getting adopted should've been a breeze."

But it hadn't been. For whatever reason, adoption hadn't been in the cards. And he'd remained at the orphanage and things had been okay when he'd been three and four and five. Even six. But then came the series of foster homes, with their endless array of too many kids, too little food, hand-me-downs and abuses, both big and small. He'd hated every minute of them. Ran away as much as he could, because he'd actually preferred living on the streets most of the time.

"The last home...I was fourteen. Hadn't shot up yet. Barely got enough food to keep me going and I had anger, but not a lot of muscle. "There were two sixteen-year-olds in the house. They'd been there for a year. They kind of ran the place, because the foster mother was barely there."

"It was just about the money for her," Shane said angrily. Keith nodded. It wasn't fair to paint all foster families with that brush, but the kids who were tough to place...well, they were tough to place, and CSE couldn't afford to get picky about them.

"One night, they came into my room. I hadn't said anything about being gay but...they saw me, followed me one night when I went with this guy. He paid me for a blowjob and fed me and gave me money. So these guys... they took the money."

His voice was almost ready to give out, and he stopped. Shane's eyes looked wet but he didn't say anything, wouldn't have pushed Keith further. Which meant he had to go on. "They took the money. And that pissed me off but that would've been fine. But they didn't leave. Locked the door. Held me down…"

His breath was shaky and he couldn't finish now, saw the scene unfold and didn't want to fight off a panic attack. There had been one too many in this house tonight.

"You were raped, Keith."

Keith shrugged, like it didn't matter, but fuck it all, of course it did. Shane bent down and kissed him lightly, then traced Keith's lips with a finger. "You're so fucking strong—Reed and I know that. But you don't always have to be with us."

"I know that. I like to be. I just want you to know what you're getting. You might think that Reed's the most fucked-up one of this group, but—"

"You're the most quietly fucked up," Shane finished. "Brat."

"Yeah. Your brat, though."

"Yeah," Keith echoed as Reed's hand snaked across his chest and landed on top of Shane and Keith's. It remained there even as Reed snored lightly. The three of them, connected.

"I can be there for you, Keith. Whatever, however you need it. Even when you think you don't," Shane told him.

"I can't believe I shared that with you. Fifteen years with Bobby, and I could never…" He paused, caught his breath.

"I don't know why I thought he might not be able to handle it."

"Maybe he couldn't have. Sometimes, we tell people things because we think they want to know, but we're really doing it for ourselves."

"So I was selfish by telling you."

"Yeah. But I like that kind of selfishness."

Reed was still in a peacefully deep sleep between them. Keith covered him with a blanket, and he and Shane moved closer to him, neither one remotely tired. Or maybe they were just waiting up to guard Reed from his nightmares.

Either way, it was comfortable. Easier than Shane ever thought something like this could be. "He seems better," he commented.

"He's getting there."

"He's lucky to have you."

"You helped, Shane. More than you know."

Shane nodded, then asked, "What happened to him?" Keith glanced at Reed. "You really want to know?"

"No, but I need to."

18

Reed heard the men on either side of him, and even though he knew he couldn't stop the dream from coming full force, he was safe between them. They would rescue him when it got too bad. But one thing about this dream, it always had to run its course.

And he felt his body go stiff, straight, mimicking what happened to him during that horrible time, locked inside a literal box of coffin-like proportions, a vent cut out above his mouth, covered with enough mesh so he couldn't tell night from day. All six of them, plus seven hours, fifty-three minutes and twenty-nine seconds before the lid was lifted and a member of his Delta Team stared down at him with tears in his eyes.

They thought you were dead, he realized, and at times he thought so as well, even though he'd never given up hope. But realistically, you could only survive like this for so long.

He'd been lucky to have been captured during the rainy season. The water gushed in, sometimes threatening to drown him, but it kept him alive.

He wanted to walk but his arms and legs wouldn't work. Prophet, the FNG, lifted him out and carried him to the waiting helo where the medics declared him dehydrated and malaria-ridden but otherwise healthy.

Physically anyway. Because at first, the lack of sleep nearly killed him. The docs finally had to drug him in order to get him into REM. He'd hated it, because he couldn't climb out of the nightmares, had to remain there, pathetic, scared, silently screaming for help.

He'd agreed to sleep willingly—fifteen-minute intervals at first. Finally, he worked up to an hour at a time.

Of course, he was declared unfit for active duty, and since riding a desk had never been his thing, he poured himself into med school. He hadn't practiced much until Bobby and Keith encouraged him to work at the local hospital.

But they'd also brought him into their business of saving people, once they'd thoroughly saved him.

He was pretty well past panic attacks by the time he'd landed—drunk, sick, lost, on their doorway that Christmas Eve.

And he was for sure lost. Barely sleeping, pretending he had it all together when he was really white-knuckling it through every damned day.

Of course, they'd seen right through the bravado act that reappeared as soon as the fever fled. Bobby took him in hand first, let Reed think he was controlling the situation by initiating the sex. But Bobby had been in charge, had just proven it more subtly than Keith. Had handled him like the skittish animal he was, reeled him in and let Keith put the finishing touches on him.

After Keith fucked him and there was no mistaking that he'd been tied down and thoroughly fucked—Keith had untied him and made love to him.

For Reed that was harder than anything, because he didn't think he deserved the tenderness Keith had shown him. He'd done it again the next night, spending time poring over Reed's body until he shook and begged and came, and then slept against Keith for six hours straight.

He'd woken up in a haze of screaming, settled down with both men's hands on him and spilled his story.

It wasn't a total, instant miracle but a minor one—the sleeping and helping him get his shit together, along with laughter and sex. The offer of a job so he could be useful again.

And then he asked if he could stay in their lives. They told him they'd been planning on asking him anyway.

Reed started to yell almost as soon as Keith finished telling the story, but Shane followed Keith's lead and touched him with a heavy pressure. Keith whispered, Shane caught Reed's hand in his and within moments, the deep, easy breathing was back, along with the hint of a smile.

"Better," Keith said.

"How long?" he asked then. He was trying to picture the scene but he couldn't. It was torture—beyond, because they'd left him for dead when he didn't break after forty-eight hours.

If you could survive that long, they felt as if the window of opportunity closed.

"Six days plus some."

Keith knew the exact hours—Shane was sure Reed remembered it to the second but both men were still trying to spare him.

It was as endearing as it was frustrating.

"He's okay, Shane. He really is. But you can't get out of something like that without a lifetime of scars."

"How did he get this far?"

"He kept moving," Keith answered simply. "When things get really bad, you don't have the luxury of choice. You just keep moving forward, like you did."

At Keith's words, Shane realized he smiled. "I guess I did."

Reed finally woke and stretched a full twelve hours later. Shane and Keith had taken turns staying with him, and now it was Shane's turn. He'd showered, his hair was still damp, and he wore the borrowed clothes as he watched a movie and Reed.

"Welcome back," he said quietly, for lack of anything better.

Reed gave him a lazy smile and accepted the can of Coke

Keith had brought in a few minutes earlier, like he'd known Reed would stir soon.

Obviously, Keith knew everything about everything.

Reed put a hand on his cheek and rubbed, murmured, "Don't look so worried. I'm okay." And then he added, "You okay with what happened last night?"

Shane couldn't bite back his smile. "Hell yeah."

"Good. And I'm guessing Keith told you what that PTSD crap was all about," Reed said.

"He did. I guess you understood my nightmares way better than I thought."

"Then why do you still look apprehensive?"

"I don't know much about you," Shane admitted.

"You know what I look like when I come. You know I like to be spanked. I'd say you know some of my deepest, darkest secrets. The rest is just frosting, but hell, if you want to know, you're welcome to the rest of my life."

Shane smiled at the easiness with which Reed was going to give that information up, although he supposed after learning what he had, the rest of it will be easy enough. "I'd like that."

Reed stuck out his hand for Shane to shake. "Johnny Lou Reed from Mobile, Alabama." His twang was deep, his smile wide, and Shane could see the young boy, all legs and charm causing all kinds of mischief.

"What about your parents?"

"Alive and well and married for fifty years. My sisters

and their babies live in Mobile still, right in the same neighborhood where we grew up. They know I'm gay, don't know about Delta, and they love me. Wish I visited more. They're both still practicing small-town medicine and my mom also got her veterinary license. She's an overachiever."

"Guess that runs in the family."

Reed touched his nose and then pointed at Shane. "They visit here every couple of years. They're actually due to come here this spring."

A hit of nerves jangled through Shane. Meeting the parents had never exactly gone well for him. When Kyle's parents met him, they'd acted like he didn't exist, like Kyle wasn't really gay, even though the man had been telling them so since he'd been fifteen.

"Kyle's parents never liked me. They thought his being gay was a phase. They thought that I was stopping him from moving on to marry his high school sweetheart."

"He had a high school sweetheart?" Reed asked. "Yeah, Paul Nickels. Prom king."

Reed laughed long and loud at that. "I know I would've loved your Kyle."

19

"Time for more training—and this time, I'm not going to go easy on you," Keith called in to where Shane had been sitting on the couch, watching TV, half bored out of his mind.

"Yeah, you've been so sweet to me," he retorted, and the man quirked his lips.

He followed Keith into the training room. Three days had passed since Reed had come home and that had been a whirlwind. Reed and Keith spent two days helping someone through their mission, and Shane had remained on the periphery, watching and waiting, in case they needed help.

They hadn't. He'd felt slightly disappointed and more than a little unsure of himself. They'd come pretty far in a short time...and now, he felt as though they'd taken several steps back.

Reed had been out all day on house calls. And Shane had actually been surprised that Keith had called for him.

Surprised, but the command wasn't unwelcome. He trudged toward the training room, wearing shorts and a

T-shirt, feet bare and found Keith only wore shorts. Hadn't bothered putting on protective gear but he'd insisted Shane wear it. And Shane did, put it all on and then stripped it off just as fast.

"What the hell's going on, Shane?"

"You're still going easy on me," he said, realizing his frustration was coming from a totally different place.

"I like rough," Keith told him.

"What makes you think I don't?" Shane demanded. "You're acting like I can't handle you."

"Can you?" Keith folded his arms and waited.

"Why are you always testing me, goddammit?" he roared suddenly, without warning. Pushed Keith hard against his chest with both hands and then used his leg to take the man to the ground. Keith went down hard, cursing, and he retaliated instantly. Within seconds, the men were brawling, military style. Wrestling. Fighting for their reputations, fighting through their anger.

He flipped Keith and straddled his back. And Keith went still, turned his head and rested it on his arms.

"You might be able to handle me," he commented blithely, and just like that, the anger went out of Shane.

He stared at the man's broad back, had wanted to trace the muscles in Keith's back for weeks. Now, that opportunity presented itself, and he wasn't stopping. He put his hands on Keith's shoulders as if to hold him down, trailed kisses down the man's neck and spine, stopping to run his tongue along his shoulder blades.

Keith's body shuddered under the touch. After Shane finished there, he continued along, licking, sucking, biting.

He bit the man on the shoulder, hard enough to leave a nice red mark…and then he sucked it so it stood out more.

"You're marking me?" Keith sounded surprised and pleased. Shane figured he'd leave the other shoulder for Reed, and there was so much more he wanted to do.

Keith had ideas of his own, spun around and flipped Shane because he'd been too caught up in admiring his handiwork. But being trapped under Keith's body—it was okay.

Keith had his wrists trapped over his head in one of his hands, and was doing some marking of his own, biting, sucking, licking—started around his pecs and then bit a nipple again and again because Shane gasped and subsequently cursed every time.

"Bastard," Shane told him.

"Yes," Keith said with the grin of someone who'd been called that many times in his life—enjoyed the moniker more than he should. "You seem to like it."

"Fuck yeah," he breathed.

Keith ground their cocks together, and Shane wanted to be naked. Immediately. He tried to make those needs known, but Keith was taking his sweet time.

"Come on, man."

"You think begging will get you anywhere?"

"Worth a try." Shane rocked his hips up, and Keith covered his mouth with a long, hot kiss that let Shane know which of them was running the show. Fuck it. He surrendered into it, because the pleasure promised to be intense.

Finally, Keith's fingers slid inside of him, two of them, well lubed, twisting. He put his head back and just sighed with pleasure, and Keith nipped at the skin along his collarbone. Then the big man slid down, began suckling Shane's balls, first one then the other as his fingers worked in and out, brushing Shane's prostate.

The tease wasn't over. Keith was showing his dominance, and at this point, Shane really had no choice but to take it. Enjoy it. Lose himself in it.

Keith slid a third finger inside of him, and Shane stilled at the new intrusion.

Keith was big, was preparing him for a nice, long fuck.

"All right?" Keith asked as the monumentality hit Shane.

"Yeah," he breathed out and Keith passed a knuckle over his gland over and over again. Shane was aware he was incoherently begging and pleading, until Keith commanded, "Flip over—hands and knees. Spread yourself for me," and Shane heard himself whimper as he did so, ass in the air, elbows down, opened to whatever the hell Keith decided to do to him.

With him.

And then Keith's tongue flicked over his hole, and he

cursed loudly enough that, if there had been neighbors, they definitely would've heard. Keith did it over and over, until his tongue worked its way inside Shane, the nerve endings inside in his channel on pleasurable fire.

And then, with little warning, he mounted Shane and began pushing his cock in. He'd used lube on the condom, but it would still hurt. Shane welcomed it, wanted it. Keith felt huge inside of him, remained still for only a long moment, didn't seem to care about giving Shane time to adjust, just seemed intent on moving. Fucking. Rutting.

His knees stung, his ass took every inch Keith gave him as he buried his head in his hands and let Keith take him. Keith pressed down on Shane's lower back, making him arch and take the big man in deeper, so he felt Keith's cock in his tonsils.

Keith lay next to Shane. He'd thrown a towel down so they wouldn't stick so badly to the mat, and Shane was on his side, curled. A flush had spread across his cheeks from exertion, but now he looked contented.

"Next time, I won't give in that easily," he promised, and Keith laughed, long and loud, stared up at the ceiling before turning his gaze back to the anything-but-submissive man next to him.

Anything but submissive, except to Keith. Keith welled with pride at the thought of being the one Shane could submit to, maybe the only one he ever had, if he'd read the situation correctly.

"You submitted to me," Keith said, checking his assumption. "How badly were you faking it?"

"You'd have known if I was." Shane's voice was rough as he spoke.

"I'd like to think so. Nothing wrong with the need to switch. Best of both worlds, if you ask me."

"It wasn't as hard as I thought. I guess I needed it, just like you said. You sensed it, even though I was less than forthcoming." Shane hung his head but Keith put a hand under his chin and brought his face up. When he saw the understanding in Keith's eyes, all Shane could say was, "Thank you."

"For what?"

"For letting me be strong when I needed to be. For letting me be weak when I needed to be."

"Baby boy, there's nothing weak about submission when you need it, and you know it. You're only weak if you can't ask for what you need," Keith told him. "You ask and you get."

"I did," Shane said. "I've gotten everything I need here. I don't want to leave."

"So don't."

"You'd really…after everything I told you, you'd let me…"

"Not let, want," Keith corrected. "The door's open."

Shane felt tears rise and he shoved them down ruthlessly.

He had to get rid of Guthrie, get rid of his past in order to save his future.

But without that past, you'd never have found this.

"Do you miss the Marines?" he asked.

"Sure. I loved it. But working private lets me cut through some of the red tape. And I'm still supporting my country." He paused. "I was a good Marine, but I work better without restrictions."

"But sometimes, everyone needs that. So who reins you in?"

"Used to be Bobby," Keith offered. "Now, it's mainly me reining Reed in."

"Maybe there's someone now who can rein you in," Shane pointed out, his words quiet but the smirk unmistakable.

"Maybe there is."

The Shane sitting across from him was a different man from the one who'd showed up on their doorstep. He was cool, confident, had a sardonic grin that might be misinterpreted by most. He'd no doubt been born with it, the grin only given when he was relaxed.

"I can't believe I didn't peg you correctly," Keith said.

"You were close. Had a right to be suspicious," Shane told him.

He was still a little thin, which was why Keith kept on feeding him any chance he got.

Kyle's death had thrown Shane for a loop. Taken the drive out of him. But it was back now, and Kyle would've approved where he ended up. Maybe even had a hand in it.

Hey, Keith kept saying there was magic to this place he didn't understand.

Keith showered and headed to the office, was surprised to find Reed already there.

"Didn't hear you come in."

"Not surprised," Reed said, his voice tight, clipped, and Keith started. He'd been pretty absorbed in fucking Shane, so no, he hadn't noticed Reed come in— or felt Reed watching.

"Why didn't you say anything?"

"Like what?"

"Like, mind if I join you?"

"Now I have to ask?"

"What? No...what the fuck is going on here, Reed?" Keith demanded. "Nothing," Reed mumbled. His cheeks were slightly flushed, and Keith moved closer to him, suddenly realizing, "You're jealous." Reed shrugged.

"You're the one who wanted this."

Reed shook his head miserably and stared out the window next to him, as if he couldn't look Keith in the eyes. "Yeah, I know."

Reed was jealous and it was absolutely the last emotion Keith had expected from the man.

"Don't." Reed held up a hand as if warding Keith off, but upsetting Reed was never something he worried about— because getting Reed upset was the only way to get him past it and moving upwards.

Keith caught his scarred wrist, always hidden by the leather bracelet of Bobby's he'd worn since practically his first month here. Now, Keith took it off and rubbed the scar that felt far worse than it looked, reminded again about how lucky Reed had been not to lose his hand or damage it forever. Which might've interfered with his medical career.

"Don't," Reed said again, his voice a little lower this time.

"Come on, baby. You were the one who knew it was right from the first. Your instincts are always right, as much as it pains me to admit it."

"Will you put that in writing?" Reed asked, and Keith brought his hand up to his mouth, kissed the inside of his wrist. "Fuck, your instincts were right too, you know."

"Well, of course," he said immodestly.

"Bastard."

"Just the way you like me."

"I feel like—"

"A red-blooded American man," Keith said. "I was jealous too. Still am. You opened up to him so easily."

"And then so did you," Reed said sharply.

"Reed...baby—please." Keith turned his face with a hand cupping his chin. "There's no replacing you—I don't want to replace you."

"Yeah, I know. It's just...it's been a while. I forgot the dynamics. How it can be in the beginning."

"I was jealous as hell when you and Bobby started

fucking," Keith reminded him, and yeah, the man had been a bear, had often taking his worry and frustration out on Reed when it was their turn.

And Reed had loved it—responded to the rough-and-tumble fucking—had made Keith fall in love with him equally as hard as Bobby had fallen with him.

"I guess there's room for all of us," Reed said finally.

"Of course there is, if that's what you want. And if you don't—"

"What? You'd let him go?" Reed asked.

"I'd do anything for you, Reed, you know that. But you need to tell me now, before we get in any deeper. And if we decide to move forward, you can never ask me that again," Keith warned.

"I know. That wasn't fair." Reed shifted in his chair and pulled something out of a drawer. "I found this yesterday."

Keith opened the envelope and read the contents. Now, he understood where Reed's admissions were coming from—this was enough to set anyone on edge. "We'll take care of this."

"We have to. And I don't want him to go. Never did."

"I know. You're just…"

"Scared to be with him alone," Reed finished for him. "And how fucking ridiculous is that?"

"It's not," Keith told him softly. "I don't want to screw this up."

"You're not. I want you to be comfortable. I thought you

were."

"Yeah, I did too. And it's not Shane's fault. It's mine." Reed took the envelope back. "No matter what, we have to deal with this, and fast."

"I think we should wait to tell him."

"You think he'll run?" Reed asked softly. "Yeah. I think he would now."

Reed looked at the envelope in his hand and then dropped it back into the drawer. "Then we make sure he's ready to stay before we show him."

Several weeks passed in a heartbeat. Keith went on another mission, Shane helped to track him this time, along with a very restrained Reed. At first, Shane chalked it up to stress but he had to wonder if Reed wasn't happy that Shane had slept with Keith.

"Hey Shane, can you come here a minute?" Keith called from the living room. Shane was in the kitchen, grabbing a soda. He looked out the kitchen door and saw them standing together, trying to look like everything was completely normal, and they sucked at it.

They had something to tell him—it was about as fucking obvious as the snow outside. But Shane steeled himself for whatever it was. He was getting stronger. Training twice a day to get back into prime condition. And he almost had himself fooled that everything was going to be all right.

"What's up?" he asked, pretending he was all fine. "We have something to show you," Reed said.

Keith walked over to him and held out an envelope. Shane took it, forced himself to draw a breath before he opened it.

"Tell him to stay quiet, and none of you will have any problems."

Guthrie. He'd been here, to Shane's sanctuary. He'd threatened the men who'd saved him.

"When?" he asked quietly, and when he got no answer, he demanded, "When, dammit? How long ago?"

"Three weeks ago," Keith told him. He looked at Reed, who was stonily silent.

"Three weeks? And I suppose you think you had a good reason why you didn't tell me?"

"Several, actually. I just don't think you're going to be able to get over yourself long enough to hear them."

Keith was right about that but Shane didn't care. Shoved away from Keith's touch to his shoulder. He was angry. Prepared to fight.

"Shane, we wouldn't have let him get to you," Reed told him.

"Now you're talking to me?" he asked, and Reed flinched. "Yeah, you think I'm walking around here in some kind of cloud, not noticing shit? I notice everything. And this—" he held up the letter, "—is my ticket out of here."

"I didn't think you wanted out," Reed said.

"It doesn't matter what I want. This dictates where I go. And you should've told me when it happened."

"You weren't ready to deal with it," Keith said.

"You don't get to make those decisions for me,

goddammit," he roared, and Keith crossed his arms and stared him down. "Just because I've given you my submission in the bedroom doesn't mean I'm going to give it to you in every area of my life."

"I didn't say you had to," Keith said. "So what exactly would you have done? Gone after Guthrie before you were well enough? Let him ruin your recovery and your possible happiness? Tell me, Shane, what you would've done three weeks ago besides freak the fuck out."

Keith spoke calmly and that pissed Shane off more than anything. He was spinning, the roar in his ears was like an oncoming hurricane pounding through his brain. Before he knew it, he'd pushed the big man squarely in the chest, over and over.

The man didn't move, stood like an elephant being bothered by a fly. It pissed Shane off when all he wanted was an I'm sorry, any kind of goddamned reaction instead of the ever-present smugness. Pissed him off even more than Reed did at the moment and, for whatever reason, it was safer to go off on Keith for now.

Finally, he got his wish. Keith's patience expired and he did explode, pinned him to the floor, rubbed his scruff against Shane's cheek. "You want a reaction, baby boy, you've got it. I didn't want you to be any more hurt than you were. I wanted to protect you, although when you act stupid like this, it's hard to remember why."

"Then teach me."

Keith's body went tight on his. "You want a lesson?"

"Yes." He put his forehead against the carpet, his eyes stung with tears of humiliation. "I need it."

He never thought he'd hear himself ask for it, but it was the only way he could possibly calm the hell down. His body still strummed with anger, unreasonable but unmoving.

"Are you doing this because you think we won't keep you any other way?" Reed asked him, and Shane didn't answer. Because this might be his last time with Keith— with both of them—and he'd be damned if he was going to say anything that might stop it.

"Fuck, he's stubborn," Keith grunted, and yes, he was, but he was no match for the angrier Marine at this moment.

He was over Keith's lap, pants down. He heard Reed's sharp intake of breath as he watched.

Reed was going to watch. Shane's brain finally caught up and he tried to move, to take it back, to run, but Keith wasn't letting him go. A strong hand came down with a slap on his ass, and he yelled—a curse surrounding Keith's name, renaming him something like motherfucking Keith.

It didn't stop Keith. In fact, the slaps came faster, harder, in a pattern that might've made sense to Keith but made none to Shane, so he was unable to steel himself against the blows since he had no clue where they'd hit or how.

He squirmed, ashamed of how hard he was, realized quickly he was on the brink of coming. And then he realized that no one was stopping him from doing so—

from enjoying that—but him. And as soon as he let that go, he let his climax take him over, his body writhing and Keith's strong hands holding him in place.

As soon as he could see—and breathe in more than just pants—Keith helped him off his lap, and he sank to his knees. He leaned against Keith's thigh, and Reed came over, got on his knees and embraced him.

"I'm here for you, Shane. I know it hasn't seemed like it, but I am," Reed murmured against his cheek. And then he turned Shane's head and kissed him.

"I'm angry that I let Guthrie run me off."

"You were reeling from grief. You didn't want to mix revenge into that, because that would ruin your memories."

It was so simple when Keith explained it. "How do you know shit like that?"

"I read people." Now, it was as much a part of him as breathing—it was his life and his job. But growing up, it had equaled survival. "You're good at it."

"I have to be." An emotion flashed across Keith's face, one Shane hadn't remembered seeing before. He put a hand on Keith's forearm, asked, "You okay?"

"Maybe. Been a long winter. A good winter, and it's not over yet." His voice was gruff, and the only thing Shane could think of to do was kiss him, a long, deep kiss until he felt Keith surrender, sink into it.

21

Shane showered, letting the water sluice down his body. He felt satiated and tense all at once, and he knew the time had come to put everything on the table. Keeping it back from Keith and Reed would make things so much worse.

He stared out the window, noting that the snow had tapered off. This was the time to go, to run. To keep running.

And where will that get you?

Besides, he'd finally found home, and he wasn't giving it up that easily.

He went to them. They were sprawled on the couch together, and Reed looked slightly unsure, like he was wondering if they'd pushed Shane too hard. And that made him feel guiltier than ever.

"Come sit, Shane, sit with us. We'll talk about this, figure it all out," Reed told him now.

"I can't," Shane told him.

"You need to learn to ask for what you want," Keith said.

"I need to tell you the truth," Shane told them, and Keith's eyes widened in response for just a second before he brought his attention to neutral. "Okay? Get it—I don't want to but I need to. And if you kick me the hell out because of it…it wouldn't matter because I'd have done the right thing, and goddammit, I've always tried to."

Reed sat like stone.

"I, ah, need to talk to you both about Guthrie," he started, and he didn't know if it was his tone or the look on his face, but both men sat up quickly. Keith didn't stop there, stood and faced Shane. "I didn't tell you the whole truth."

"And what's that?" Reed drawled, his voice low and honeyed and equally dangerous.

Shane braced himself. "I'm not…Army. That was part of my cover."

Reed's shoulders sagged and Keith said one word, his tone clipped. "Spook."

"Yes," Shane agreed. "I'm not a Ranger. I'm CIA. Ex-CIA. I've been burned." He heard Keith blow out a slow whistle, heard Reed mutter something about Keith being right about things.

"So, what, if the sex hadn't gone well, you would never have given us the truth, just disappeared into the night?" Keith asked.

"I knew it would go well before any of that. Before I watched you two. It was in the way you took care of me. You broke me."

"Ah, so it's our fault."

"Yes." Shane was convinced of it, so much so that Keith

had to fight the urge to both laugh and hug the kid. But it wasn't the time for that now. This was serious business, the-truth's-going-to-fling-you-around-like-a-goddamned-hurricane time.

"And what about Guthrie? Because that note was real," Keith said.

"He's real—he's CIA. And he did kill Kyle, and he is after me. He burned me."

"How convenient that some of the truth fit in with your goddamned lies," Reed railed. "And you thought nothing of betraying us. Nothing."

"I didn't...fuck, you can't believe I betrayed you. Please, Reed, you of all people."

"You took my trust and fucking killed it," Reed said bitterly, right before he walked out.

Keith put a hand on the back of Shane's neck. "He'll come around."

"Doesn't feel like it," Shane said. "I really fucked up. Again."

"Fear makes us do strange things."

At one time, Shane would've bet that Keith would be the angry one, stomping away at this reveal, but no, Reed was always the one who'd feel the betrayal keenly. His emotions were always right on the surface, sometimes too close for comfort.

"You had to tell us. You did the right thing," Keith reassured him. Again, he repeated, "Doesn't feel like it."

"There's more going on here than just you not telling us," Keith admitted. "Getting three men together like this doesn't happen without some strife."

"I'm breaking you guys apart," Shane said. That had been his biggest fear, right behind not wanting him to stay.

"You're not."

Keith's arms crossed, waiting and watching as Shane shifted nervously. Could be an act…but it could also mean the whole truth was finally coming. And if he was a betting man, he'd bet on the latter.

Shane bowed his head for a long minute and then pulled himself up and met Keith's eyes. "I was recruited out of boot camp by the CIA. Sent to the farm and reinfiltrated through Ranger school because there were several high-ranking Rangers selling munitions in third-world countries."

"Go on."

"Guthrie killed Kyle—that part's all too goddamned true." His eyes clouded but his gaze never left Keith's face.

"You're paid to lie."

"Yes, but you have to understand why I couldn't tell you the truth. It was too fucking dangerous."

"Isn't it still?" Keith asked and Shane nodded. "So why reveal it all now?"

"Because I don't want to leave. But you deserve to know how much trouble I'm bringing with me. Staying here isn't my decision anymore. I can't have another death on my conscience."

Reed heard it all, his suspicions finally confirmed. There was nothing he could've presented as evidence—it was simply a matter of a special forces operator knowing one of his own kind, whether it be solider or spy. Shane's abilities seemed to extend beyond Ranger training. When Shane had helped to save Keith when he was in South America, Reed had known something was up. But he was also a patient man.

"Reed, I know you're listening," Shane called. Reed opened the door, leaned against the jamb.

"Fuck, don't look at me like that. I didn't betray you."

"Yeah, you did." Reed was surprised at the hurt in his voice. "I didn't bring Guthrie here."

"You used us as a safe house," Reed shot back. "And you didn't let us prepare," Keith added. "Are you kidding? This place is a fortress."

"You know as well as I do that mental prep's the most important thing," Keith growled.

"I tried to goddamned leave, remember?" Shane leaned back against the wall, knocked his head against it lightly a few times. "Do you want me to go now? If it means keeping you safe, making you trust me, fuck, I'll do anything."

"I want you to tell us the entire truth," Keith said. "Okay."

"Come into the kitchen and sit. I have a feeling it's going to be a long explanation," Reed said tiredly.

"I'd do anything to wipe that look off your face," Shane told him, then followed the men to the kitchen.

Keith passed coffee mugs around the table. There was silence for several long moments as he and Reed sat and Shane continued to stand.

Finally, Shane sat heavily and began speaking almost immediately. "Shane Wills, aka Malcolm Parker. Parents unknown. Birthdate unknown but estimated." He rattled off a date that would make him twenty-nine. Older than they'd thought, which made sense, given the spooking thing and the fact that his last assignment hadn't been his first.

"Foster care," Keith said.

"Yes. I enlisted at seventeen. A judge signed off on it because I was already emancipated from the foster-care system and I was trying to erase a lot of petty crimes I'd gotten caught for off my record."

"Which means there's a long list of non-petty crimes you didn't get caught for," Keith said, and Shane smiled that I-could-charm-the-pants-off-anyone smile, indicating how right Keith was.

You're supposed to be pissed at him, he reminded himself, but that seemed to be a mission impossible.

"I went into the Army intending to be part of the Rangers. Halfway through boot camp, a guy approached me. He was a CIA director. They were actively recruiting and I ended up on their radar for a number of reasons."

Shane wasn't ready to share exactly what that skillset was, but he would, especially when Prophet started using him on jobs.

"So you went to Quantico," Reed said.

"Yep. They took me to the farm after I'd been in the Army for six months, trained the hell out of me and sent me back to become a Ranger. At first, I infiltrated a small battalion accused of selling arms. A good mission. Successful. But that was just the tip of the iceberg, and I knew it was a long-term undercover mission. I stayed in the field for a couple of years."

"And during all of this, you were with Kyle," Reed said quietly.

"Yeah." Shane's face grew somber. "Met him in Afghanistan, of all places. I didn't lie about any of that. Two years together. We lived together too, mainly because I was living out of a suitcase for those years."

"How much did Kyle know?"

"He thought I was a Ranger, plain and simple. I deceived him."

"You did your job. Protocol's in place for your safety and the safety of your family and friends," Reed said.

"And look how much it helped."

Reed couldn't argue that. "Keep going, Shane."

Shane's eyes flicked between Reed's and Keith's.

"Everything I told you about Kyle was true—the explosion, him leaning over me…the gunshot. At least, I thought it was."

He wasn't going to be able to go on, and suddenly, Reed understood why. Shane was staring at his wrists, the scars, and yes, there was more to this story and it involved far more torture than Shane had ever let on.

Reed could be unforgiving, but not about something like this. He'd been right from the start—he and Shane were more alike than even he'd known.

Shane had lied because dealing with the truth might rip him apart, bring him back to that place of darkness. Clawing his way up out of that hole was the hardest thing he'd ever done. Doing it a second time…well, he might not make it.

His arms were on the table in front of him. He heard a click and Reed's heavy watch came off and thunked onto the wood table. A snap and the leather bracelet he wore on the other wrist was off too.

Shane looked up questioningly and then down again as Reed put a wrist on either side of Shane's.

It was only then that Shane saw the band of scars that matched his own. They were lighter but still visible. Reed turned his hands wrists-up so Shane could see the circles all the way around.

"These gave me away from day one," he said in a choked voice. "You ended up in the right house," was Reed's answer to that.

Keeping his eyes glued to the scars in front of him, Shane spoke. His voice sounded far away, as if he were going back to that not-so-distant time and place whether he wanted to or not.

"Guthrie chained me down so I couldn't help Kyle," he said. "Kyle wasn't shot?"

"Not with a bullet," Shane said. He just hadn't finished the story, because that's where he'd wished the horror had ended, that Kyle had died a quick, peaceful death. "Guthrie thought he knew things about the munitions. He didn't—I know he didn't. But Guthrie didn't believe me. Told me I was too close to the situation. Now I realize that Guthrie thought Kyle was on to him."

"Because Guthrie had gotten involved with the Rangers who were selling the guns?" Keith asked and Shane nodded.

"I didn't realize it at first myself. Not until that night."

"What happened after you thought Guthrie killed Kyle?" Keith prompted and Shane didn't want to go there, didn't want to think about the cell ever again.

He'd woken, blinked at the flickering lights. Smelled the dank dampness of an underground room and struggled to sit up. But his wrists were chained to either side of him, the chains bolted to the wall.

He'd tugged to see how much hold they had. Realized

he was going nowhere fast, but when the screaming from the next room started, it didn't matter. For hours, Kyle screamed and begged, and Shane tried to get free, wouldn't have cared at that point if his arms ripped off.

He'd pulled every muscle. Dislocated his shoulders, broken both wrists. Dug the metal bands so deeply into his skin that they were practically embedded. He could still hear them separating from the infected skin when the medic freed him, not knowing the extent of the damage he was inflicting.

He remembered not screaming when it was done. Didn't need to, because he could still hear Kyle's screaming inside his head.

"Guthrie…I don't know what he did to Kyle. I stayed up nights imagining…and they wouldn't let me see the body. I never saw him again." Except in every dream he'd had since it happened.

"Who rescued you?" Reed asked.

"Rangers. They thought the rebels did it because of a gun deal gone bad. I was too weak to tell anyone it was Guthrie. By the time I could…" He shook his head but didn't finish the thought.

"You didn't tell because you wanted revenge on Guthrie for yourself," Keith said.

Shane nodded. "I had to get myself together in order to do it. I needed…time."

The room was so silent. Shane didn't want to look

up, couldn't keep staring at the scars. He forced his eyes upwards, met Keith's first.

His expression was the softest Shane had ever seen. Shane's shoulders sagged in relief, and something that had been strung so tight for so long released. The tears ran hot down his face, and he was aware of Reed moving closer. Of arms circling him. Of a strong hand clasping his.

"You're together now, and you're not alone," Reed whispered. "Took me a long time to realize that having people by your side is the only way to really live."

After a long while, the tears dried. Darkness fell. Shane was guided into the bedroom. Tucked in, with two bodies pressed against his. For tonight, they would guard against the nightmares.

22

As they lay next to him, Shane fell into a deep, almost trancelike sleep, as though the truth had drained everything from him. Reed and Keith remained silent for a quite awhile, each wrapped in his own thoughts.

At one point, Keith had grabbed for the iPad, and Reed figured he was emailing Prophet the intel and waiting for an answer. And when he put the iPad down, he looked at Reed.

"So now we know." Reed heard the tightness in his voice as he spoke.

"We know he's capable," Keith said. "He didn't lie about being sick. About needing time to heal."

Reed nodded. "He wasn't telling us because he wasn't able to face the whole thing. He had to grieve for Kyle. And then, he was also worried about us— wanted to protect us. If we'd gone searching for Guthrie, we would've tipped him off and possibly brought him to our door before we were ready."

Keith nodded and Reed continued, "So we're finally

agreeing on him."

"I guess we were both right," Keith said "It all makes sense now. The sex part, I mean."

"He let you in," Reed added. "I don't think that was part of his cover."

"I think he just blew his entire cover."

"Because of us?"

"For us," Keith corrected as his iPad beeped. "There's Proph."

Reed moved to the other side of the bed so they could both talk to Proph, and Shane instinctively moved away from the empty space and closer to Keith. Keith put a hand on Shane's arm as they listened to Prophet's report.

"No CIA file," Prophet confirmed. "Which means that Shane Wills is as deadly as I am."

"Ah, Proph, you're just a big cuddly teddy bear," Reed drawled, and Prophet simply blinked at him.

"Fuck you, Johnny Lou Reed."

"Bed's already pretty crowded but I'm sure we can accommodate a guest appearance." Reed propped his hand in his chin. "We can trust him."

"Yeah, you can. Because he's been more fucked over by that agency than I was. I've got a few ideas about helping him, but—"

"We need to let Guthrie find him," Reed finished.

"That'd be the best way. No fuss, no muss," Prophet agreed. "Guthrie's real name is Spicer. Fun fact, he's actually the son of the director who recruited Shane—I was still in when that happened. I knew the father and the asshole son."

"Well, let's put that on a Snapple bottle cap," Keith muttered. "So this is definitely no accident," Reed said, ignoring him. "I'd bet my life no," Prophet agreed.

"So they thought Shane would be a patsy and were surprised when he turned out to be an excellent agent?" Keith asked. "Hell of a chance to take."

"What if Shane was put in to watch Guthrie? To take over for him?" Reed proposed. "What if his father underestimated his son?"

Keith sat back, steepled his fingertips together. Reed could practically see the wheels turning, and he and Prophet just waited his thoughts out. Because they were always worth waiting for.

"I need Guthrie's records. All of them," he said finally. "Why?"

"I'm betting Guthrie failed every psych eval and dear old dad's regretting ever covering it up."

"So Shane was his keeper?" Reed asked

"Shane was Guthrie's partner, whether he knew it or not," Keith said gruffly. "If Guthrie kills Shane, then he gets rid of the one man who could end him."

"What about Guthrie's father?"

"Guthrie already took care of him," Prophet confirmed. "Does Shane know that?" Reed asked.

"I'm guessing yes. Guy was his mentor. That's who you

go to when you're in trouble. When he found him dead—"

"Guthrie framed me for that murder and Kyle's," Shane confirmed sleepily. "How long have you been listening?" Keith asked as he clicked the screen off to keep Prophet's privacy for the moment.

Shane looked up at him "Does it matter? It's part of what I do."

"Were you testing us?"

"No, Keith, just…fuck, the more you guys know…"

"We can take care of ourselves," Reed said. "Is all what we said true?"

"Yes. But it took me a hell of a lot longer to figure it out. I thought Guthrie was on my side—until he wasn't. I felt like Guthrie's dad was mine—Guthrie was my brother. How fucking stupid was I?"

"Pretty stupid," Keith agreed. Reed hit him in the arm and Keith continued, "You were looking for a home. You found it with the dad and let your guard down."

You let your guard down.

That was exactly what he was doing here.

"This is different," Keith said. "But we won't just expect you to believe the words. We'll prove it to you."

Now that he knew the whole truth, Keith realized just how much trouble Shane was in. Keith stared at the boy who'd played his role over the past month and knew he hadn't been faking all of it.

"You're still off your game. Because of Kyle," he told Shane now.

"Yeah," Shane breathed. "Because of you two as well. Did you think I expected this?"

"I'm guessing no. You've got to tell your story to a friend of mine. And then we'll figure out what to do, because Guthrie's not going to stop coming for you, no matter what he says, and he's going to make a stronger move soon. Before you can run again."

"I know. I figured if I didn't say it… God, how fucking stupid am I?"

"You're not stupid. You just needed time to rebuild."

"Do you want me to leave?" he asked again, and Keith shook his head as Reed said, "No."

"I've been burned. They're worried I'll come forward, reveal what I know. They want to discredit me if they can, but they'd rather kill me. I have no handler, no one I can trust."

"But you started to trust us," Keith pointed out. "You know enough to get me in real trouble."

"We know enough, but you'll have to tell our friend everything."

"Is he a merc too?"

"Straight out of the CIA. He might hold more of a grudge against the agency than you do," Reed said. "Shane, why did you keep running?"

"Because no one's believed me."

"Until now," Keith told him. "But you're lying. You've been letting Guthrie stalk you because you kept running."

"So it's my fault?"

"Yes."

"Fuck you."

"I'd probably let you, yes," Keith said calmly. "He made a mistake—he's trying to cover his tracks. You turn and face him. Men like that only bully when they're allowed to. He killed Kyle as a warning. But it was never going to end there. Men like this don't give warnings. They kill. He's going to kill you."

"So what do I do?" Shane asked, although Keith didn't doubt he already knew the answer.

"Turn around and kill him first." Reed's voice was low and steady. The look in his eyes determined. His expression brutal. "It's you or him. I know the choice we'd make."

Shane felt something inside of him lock and load, like everything clicked into place and he finally had the strength to do what he'd needed to for months.

He knew what he had to do.

"I should've done it before he killed Kyle."

"That's not your fault. He played dirty." Keith's eyes glittered with anger. "He shot Kyle in the back. Didn't give him a fighting chance. You force Guthrie to give you one."

"I will."

"We're behind you on this, Shane."

"I don't want you to think I'm here because I have nowhere else to go," Shane said slowly, like he was choosing his words carefully. "I'm lost, I get that. But if things weren't right here, I wouldn't stay. I have a bank account with plenty of savings. I'm not broke—just without a home base at the moment. But I don't want you to think this is something I fell into easily."

"I don't think that. I think you wrestled with your grief. You just did it in an abbreviated amount of time."

"What do I do?"

"Stay here. Let us figure out how to help you."

"It's that simple?"

"It can be," Reed said.

"We'll keep you safe," Keith said.

"Whatever you need," Reed added, and Shane wanted to ask if he really meant that, but held it back.

Reed opened his eyes when he heard the groans. He'd fallen asleep on the couch watching a movie with the other men. Obviously, they'd woken already, and he looked over at the other couch, propped himself up on an elbow and watched the show sleepily.

Shane was in Keith's lap, straddling the bigger man. Maybe it was relief at having admitted everything or maybe this had always been Shane, but Reed realized how much he was enjoying this particular show. Shane taking control of Keith, holding the big man's shaved head, grinding against him until Keith was growling in frustration.

"You think you're winning this, baby boy?" he heard Keith ask, and he shivered at the man's tone of voice. He saw Shane shudder too, and yeah, Keith had that kind of command in his voice.

"I do."

Keith stood, with Shane wrapped around him. Knelt so they were both on the floor, and Shane said, "You'll come first if I suck you."

"You're on."

Oh, this ought to be good. Shane and Keith moved to lay with their heads and feet in the opposite directions, on their sides. Shane moved in first, yanking down Keith's sweats, taking his cock in his mouth as Keith tried to kick the pants off and strip Shane at the same time. But he took a minute to simply close his eyes and enjoy what Shane was doing to him, all the stress and worry from last night gone from his face.

When he opened his eyes, he looked at Reed and winked. Reed knew from experience that Shane wasn't winning this one, although, for some reason, he wouldn't mind watching Keith lose.

And that thought had him sitting up and paying attention.

Keith finally got it together, stripped Shane and was sucking him, fingering the younger man's ass as Shane jolted from the intrusion. As Reed watched the men, a tangle of limbs, their heads positioned between one another's legs, he thought he could probably come right there. Stroked himself a few times languidly, wondering how things could've been so bad at one point last night and so goddamned good right now. But this…this was right. It had taken him longer to get here than he'd thought. But he washere.

Shane was barely hanging on, as Keith spread the younger man's legs wide, was sucking his balls and using his hand to stroke up and down his cock, ensuring that Shane was nearly incoherent. But he was putting up a good fight— taking Keith's thick cock in his mouth, trying to give as good as he got.

Reed couldn't wait any longer. He moved forward, removing clothing as he walked. When he knelt by them, he moved next to Shane, in between Keith's legs.

Keith paused for a second, muttered something about both of them playing dirty, just as Reed took one of Keith's balls in his mouth and hummed.

Keith groaned around Shane's cock, and Shane continued to work Keith's cock, Reed licking under his balls, the spot he knew Keith couldn't handle for long. Within a few seconds, the big man tensed, released Shane's cock from his mouth and then yelled as he came, clutching Shane's hips to keep him close.

Shane moved his lower body away, even as his mouth continued to milk Keith, who lay with his hand over his face, his breath coming fast. Reed moved up to kiss him, and Keith responded instantly, his tongue playing with Reed's, even as the younger man rolled Keith completely onto his back and spread his legs.

He could tell by Keith's kisses exactly what Shane was doing to him, fingering him. Could feel Keith tense with one finger, then two. Glanced over and saw Shane watching them, gauging Keith's reactions, taking them seriously. Reed forced Keith to concentrate on the pleasure, stroked his cheek, felt him gradually relax as Shane brought his cock back to life. His hips rocked under Shane's hand and finally, he pulled his face away from Keith and stared down at Shane.

"It's okay. I can stop," Shane told him, but Keith shook his head. "It's not about the bet—that doesn't matter, Keith."

"It's not about the bet," Keith repeated, pulled Shane up to him. Locked his legs around Shane's waist as Shane pushed inside him. Keith moaned with his teeth gritted together, raised his head off the ground and then dropped it and breathed. Shane pushed in farther, leaned down to first kiss Keith and then Reed and finally, when he was all the way in, he angled so his thrusts could bring Keith nothing but pleasure.

"That's it, Keith—I want to hear you," he said, his voice serious, his eyes glowing.

"This is so fucking hot," Reed murmured against Keith's neck as he jerked himself, knew he'd come all over both his lovers. For that moment, they were connected, and Reed closed his eyes and thought about the magic of this cabin, the magic of the men next to him.

When he opened his eyes, Keith was coming, and both Reed and Shane were right behind him.

Reed didn't know how long they stayed on the floor, all wrapped around one another, but hell, it would never be long enough as far as he was concerned.

As Shane rolled off Keith and into the middle of the two

men, he wasn't sure what to do or say next. The fact that Keith had allowed him to do what he'd done meant the big man trusted him. Just thinking about that made him choke up.

"Talk to us, Shane," Reed urged. "I feel...desperate," he confessed.

"It's not desperate to know what you want," Reed countered. "Most people never hone in on what they really need. They're searching and then they settle, but they always feel restless. When it really clicks, you know."

It was something he never would've considered before this. Threesomes were a hot fantasy but a real-life one? How, exactly, could it work?

Worked for three men for eight years, he reminded himself.

"We've met lots of guys in the past who needed our help. Some of them stayed here without this dramatic entrance. But none of them ever came close to make us consider inviting them inside." As Reed spoke that last word, he put his fist to his heart. "So, you have to decide what it is you want, Shane."

"I want to be more than your fantasy. Because I'm goddamned real. Flesh and blood, and we all know that fantasies aren'treal."

He'd floated around for months after Kyle's death. When the threats started, they actually gave him purpose. He had to run. But now he simply felt adrift. Disconnected.

Until he collapsed on this doorstep and realized these men might just understand him.

"We weren't using you. Christ, far from it," Keith told him. "We miss Bobby, but with you, it was right. Not convenient. Right."

"I wasn't using you." But that was a lie, because he had. They'd been his crutch. But they'd also helped him to heal. Taught him to love again when he thought he'd never feel anything but pain.

"You might've been, at first. And that's all right. But I think we're past all of that. When you watched us, I think you knew. It felt electric having you there," Keith told him.

Reed just tugged Shane into his arms and said, "Life sucks a lot of the time.

Don't throw away the good parts. He'd want you to be happy, wouldn't he?" Yeah, he would, but Shane didn't trust his voice. He simply nodded and Reed smiled and said, "Then be happy."

After a long, secured session with a man called Prophet, Shane knew what he had to do, even as Prophet planned on his end. He would turn around and hunt the man who was on his six. And Keith and Reed would be there to back him up. Prophet too.

The man with the dark hair and the sardonic smile had listened to the story without saying a word, and Shane didn't know if the guy believed him. At the end, Prophet had said, "Sounds like the CIA. Bunch of asswipes."

He sounded angry—as angry as Shane felt, and he wondered how Reed and Keith had met him. But they didn't say and Shane didn't ask, supposed it would come out over time. At this moment, all that mattered was getting Guthrie the hell out of his way.

Now another week had passed, making it a month from the time Guthrie originally left the letter and nary another sign from him. But Shane didn't have a cell phone and Keith's and Reed's were secured and there was no landline for the cabin. There wasn't mail service here either—it was all delivered to a PO box in town, and Keith had checked to make sure it hadn't been compromised and that no letters had been sent.

Nothing. Keith did a search of real estate of the area and pinpointed some foreclosures that they could hone in on. But Prophet warned them away from that—telling them Guthrie would run. And they wanted him to think he had the upper hand.

But the tension was becoming unbearable, for all of them. Sitting around waiting wasn't any of their styles.

Shane was tired of sparring, of training, of pacing and waiting. Instead, he put himself on the couch in full view of the office, where Keith and Reed had been holed up all day, and stripped. Spread his legs and began to stroke himself, head back, a long sigh escaping his throat.

It had been a week since they'd touched him other than during sleep in the big bed. And he knew his nightmares were killing all of them. But they were treating him like that fragile creature who'd first landed on their doorstep—he'd have to make them stop.

When he heard them stop talking, he figured they were out of the office, watching him jerk himself off, his cock glistening with the lube he'd used to make his hand slide, the slow catch and release, the quickening of his breath. And he fucking loved this, wanted their eyes on him. Wanted to let them know that this was for them, that he was giving himself to them.

"Yeah, that's it, Shane," Keith told him, his voice hoarse. "Make it count, baby boy."

Shane groaned, threw his head back and shuddered. His cock dripped, his nipples were so damned tight they hurt, and he tugged on one. Hard.

"He'd look good pierced," Reed said, and Keith agreed. "Might have to get both his nipples done."

Jesus, they would too, would mark him up the way they wanted.

"You'd let us, wouldn't you?" Keith asked and Shane smiled, nodded, the bliss from his impending orgasm carrying him along.

"Jesus, call the piercer," Reed breathed, and with that, Shane came, spurting over his stomach, his chest as he panted and continued stroking. He noted both men were hard as anything in their pants, and he knew what he needed to do next. What he would do. And he hoped Keith would help him.

"Reed, why don't you take off your clothes? Keith can help," Shane said, and his tone was low and dangerous, maybe more so than Reed had ever heard. It melted the tension out of his body and he responded without thinking, which was exactly the way Shane wanted it.

Keith stripped his shirt, unzipped his jeans, walked Reed over to Shane. "What do you need from me, Shane?" Reed asked, sank to his knees in front of him.

"I'm going to get what I need by giving you what you need." Shane passed a hand across his lap, motioning for Reed to climb on.

Reed froze in place. Hadn't expected this at all, even though he knew that baby boy did indeed have dominant tendencies. And although he didn't have the polish Keith did, or probably the experience in clubs, he had thepresence.

Reed swallowed hard. Wanted to say don't do this, but he couldn't. Because there was no reason why Shane couldn't—no reason why Reed shouldn't want it.

Other than fear, of course. It was one thing to kiss and fuck. Another thing to trust his body like this to an unknown entity.

"I promise, you'll love it, Reed." Shane held out his hand, and Reed stood and backed up a little bit. "Don't make me come get you."

Maybe that's what he wanted, a chase to the death. Reed backed up a little more, and Keith didn't try to stop him. "I don't think I can do this."

His voice sounded strangled and he looked to Keith for help, but the bastard gave him none except that stern look that told him he wasn't getting away with anything. Shane rose off the couch and Reed told himself he was a grown fucking man, that he could stop this anytime. That he could tell them both to fuck off, use his safe word that he hadn't used in years, and they would leave him alone. Or climb into bed with him and make him feel better without all of this.

Reed opened his mouth but nothing came out. Not when Shane stood inches from him. "I'm going to ask one more time and then I'm going to drag you to the couch."

How had it come to this? Not that he hadn't been surrounded by tops all these years. Not that he hadn't known what Shane was. But he felt so damned exposed.

Shane put a hand on his cheek. "It's all okay, Reed. Come on. I know what makes you feel better. Can you trust me on this?"

Reed's shoulders slumped forward at Shane's words, and his silent surrender was seen in his short, shuffled walk to the couch, with Shane behind him. He waited until Shane sat and then he knelt, first putting his cheek against Shane's thigh, letting himself breathe through the very real possibility of the panic attack.

"Climb up, Reed." Shane's voice was so calm it was almost hypnotic. Reed did as he asked, pushed himself to lie across Shane's lap, but not before Shane asked him to take his pants down.

That was always the worst part. Bad enough when you let another man do it, but to do it yourself...it was the ultimate humiliation, because it meant you wanted it.

"Nothing to be ashamed of, Reed. You know that," Shane comforted him as he fixed himself, his cock hard despite his fear. He didn't know this boy well enough for this kind of intimacy. But obviously Shane thought he knew Reed.

The first slap came down with the right amount of pressure. Before Reed could express his surprise, several more were administered in rapid succession, until the tightness in his chest stretched to where he could barely breathe. The pressure built rapidly, and then, as it always did when Keith or Bobby was doing it, it receded, leaving him flying.

He wasn't sure how long he remained in place, but he complied easily when Shane tugged at him and said, "Come on—hands and knees now."

His body was still humming and Shane rubbed his ass, which was hot and tingling and then gave it another slap he wasn't expecting. He turned to say something but then Shane was pushing inside of him, filling him up in one long stroke that took his breath away.

"Yeah," he managed when Shane was in up to the hilt,

but the man didn't give him a second to breathe before he began to pump, hitting Reed's prostate in a way that demanded he yell. "More, Shane. I want more."

"I know. I've been told I can corrupt anyone," Shane said easily. Reed laughed as he came, Keith snorted, and they were both in deep with this one.

24

They took turns keeping watch. Shane and Reed used the ATVs to track along the perimeter, while Keith stayed at the cabin with the rifles and the NVs. According to Prophet, Guthrie was still close, although he couldn't get a bead on where the man was staying.

None of them had wanted to alert the CIA at all, because they didn't know if Guthrie still had allies there. Since the death of his father, it appeared Guthrie's stock had gone way down, but Shane took nothing for granted.

They'd done this for a week now. It was already partly in Keith and Reed's routine, so it wouldn't look all that odd to Guthrie, but they wanted to call him on, wanted to make him think he could take them down.

The thing was, he might actually be able to—at least at first. Shane had prepared himself for that eventuality, told himself that Keith and Reed would come and get him. But he woke up with nightmares every time he went to sleep these days.

Now, he rode on the ATV, seeing a few tire tracks in the

muddy snow. Used the binoculars to sight the other ATVs, noted they were driven by two young kids, just having fun. It was about to get dark, and out here, it went from dusk to black within seconds and he'd forgotten the flashlight. He turned the wheels toward the cabin, taking the route along the back, looking all around and seeing nothing. Not at first.

It was only when he got closer and caught the glint of something in the woods. He sped up, especially when he saw blood in the snow surrounding the overturned ATV.

He knew what had happened in an instant, hadn't needed to see the dart in the snow, the needle Reed had yanked out of himself, but not before it had done the damage.

Shane had always thought it would be him, hadn't prepared himself for this eventuality. He jumped off the ATV and stood, looking at the footprints and dragmarks that led deep into the woods.

He heard another ATV, turned to see Keith coming toward him.

"Guthrie drugged Reed," Shane said when Keith moved in to look at the dart with the needle.

"Bastard. Had to be stationed in the trees. Whatever was in here knocked Reed unconscious."

Which meant Guthrie had waited until the drug worked, which in turn caused Reed to crash the ATV. Hence, the blood.

"He's all right, Shane." Keith clamped a hand on his neck.

"He'd know what was happening. He didn't crash hard—it's only overturned. Look."

Shane did, so he could stop himself from hyperventilating. "We have to find Reed, Keith. I can't let him take my punishment."

Reed opened his eyes and realized he wasn't inside his nightmare. Realized too that this was much, much worse, because his real life had become the nightmare.

"Guthrie, you bastard," he grunted as he tried to move. The box was smaller than the original had been, and the drugs gave him a wicked case of vertigo.

He'd been ready to head back to the cabin when the dart caught him in the neck. He'd stopped the ATV, had planned on trying to run into the open, where Keith or Shane would've seen him, but the drug in the dart had been too strong.

He had no idea where he was or how long he'd been out—could've been hours or it could've been days.

This was his living, breathing fear and he was in it. Forced himself to breathe, to recall what he'd told Keith years earlier, after one particularly spectacular nightmare in which he managed to break Keith's nose with his flailing.

They'd discussed what they would've done differently—it was like a debriefing they did at the end of every mission, when they'd been in the military and when they were working private missions. And Reed had done his own version of a debriefing, said, "If it happened again, the box, I wouldn't struggle. It scared me, made me panic. Neither of those things did me any good. If I'd stayed quiet, they might've opened the box to see if I was alive. Maybe I could've picked the locks. Either way, I had plenty of air and water—I could've survived in there for a while."

He clung to that, to Keith nodding, telling him, "I would come get you, come hell or high water."

Using that image, and picturing Shane and Bobby, Reed hung on.

He looked up and saw a straw hanging down to him. As much as he hated being treated like a goddamned animal, survival was the most important thing. He took a pull, didn't taste any drugs and so he swallowed it. Had to be grateful that the motherfucker wasn't trying to waterboard him through the vents. Although who the hell knew what would come later. He had to be prepared for all eventualities, even the ones he didn't want to think about.

"I'm going to call Prophet."

"I'm going to have Guthrie take me," Shane told him.

Keith looked like he wanted to stop him, but finally, he relented. Slipped a GPS tracker onto the button of Shane's coat. Stared at him. "You do whatever you need to survive. Prophet and I will be tracking you every step of the way."

"I can handle this. He should never have involved Reed. This was personal."

"Still is." Keith stared at the phone in his hand and told Prophet, "He's got Reed. Here's the plan."

And then Keith got back on the ATV and took off back down to the cabin, circling around the front. Shane watched him get to the cabin and go inside.

Keith was safe. Reed wasn't. It had been over an hour since he'd last seen the man—they'd searched for him unsuccessfully before coming to the inevitable conclusion that Guthrie had planned well and they'd need to use a difference tactic. An hour would've given Guthrie enough time to hide Reed and come back. He had no phone for Guthrie to contact him. This was the only way.

Shane stood there in the freezing cold as night fell. Heard branches breaking from the ice and cold, saw his breath in front of him, the only thing he could see. An hour passed. And finally, the hair on the back of his neck rose.

He could sense Guthrie, had always been able to. One of the few perks of having worked closely with the man for a few years.

"Take me instead, you fucking bastard," Shane said quietly. His wishes were granted when a dart slammed into his shoulder and he fell to the ground as the drug entered his system in seconds.

He woke, bleary eyed, stomach churning, with a hand cuffed to a long chain attached to a wall. Just like it happened with Kyle, except this time, there was no screaming to be heard.

Shane didn't know if that was better or worse. "Guthrie, you coward! Come fight me!"

His voice echoed.

"Reed, if you're there…you're going to be fine," he told him. And then a screen above him displayed a picture. A box, with a vent on top, and Shane bent over and vomited, because he knew what Guthrie had done.

"Fucking bastard. Reed, if you can hear me, just keep breathing. I'm here. I'm not going anywhere without you."

If he'd kept track of the hours correctly, they were just entering day three, which meant that Guthrie found and discarded the GPS tracker Shane had on him and left it behind. Otherwise, Keith would be here already, wherever here was. It was around midnight, and the half-open window and lack of heat had Shane shivering and drowsy, especially because he'd been stripped down to his boxer briefs.

At some point, he'd clawed at the cuff, because the scarred skin was ripped open and bloody, but he didn't care. Had to get the fuck out of here. Had to stop falling asleep.

"Guthrie!" he yelled. Was answered by an echo of his own voice and silence. He screamed the name, over and over, until his voice was just a rasp. And then he coughed up a lung, which hurt his throat more.

"Reed, I'm okay," he managed, hoping that Reed was close and would hear him and understand. He leaned his head back as a shiver went through him, and he was dangerously drowsy again.

Something's gotta give. But would it be him?

He wasn't sure how much time passed before he blinked, because he swore he saw a glint coming in from the window above him. A skeleton key that would open his cuffs landed at his feet. He looked up, saw nothing, but knew exactly who was out there.

He also knew what was expected of him. Especially when a knife dropped down as well, still sheathed. Bobby's KA-BAR, with his name and rank inscribed along the side of it. It was heavy. Sharp. Dangerous.

This time, he would fight. And he would win. There was too much at stake not to. And as the cuff popped up, Shane stretched his body to get the sleep out of it, bounced on the balls of his feet to get his blood pumping and his head on straight. He looked at the box that was still the picture on the screen above him and whispered, "Coming for you, baby. Coming right fucking now."

And he was. He used the key to open his cell door, realized they were in some kind of basement, and based on the cold, still very much in upstate New York. He stilled in the hallway, realized that Guthrie had to have video of him, and moving forward without waiting for the confrontation could be deadly.

The knife was inside the waistband of his boxer briefs, not easily seen but would be easily pulled. He wanted Guthrie to think he was barehanded, but he had no idea if he'd seen the objects drop from the window.

He waited, his stance tight, his body warmer now that his blood was flowing pure revenge. Patience had never been his strong suit, but he'd learned it over the past months. Guthrie had been an inadvertently good teacher.

Finally, he heard the slight creak of footsteps on the stairs. He held his breath and forced himself to stay still, until the shadow fell across his path.

"Ah, Shane, do you really think you can win this?" Guthrie shook his head sadly. He carried a knife, but he closed it and slid it inside his pocket.

He doesn't even think you're worth a weapon. "Come fight me," he screamed, wanting Guthrie to think he was lost and over the edge.

Guthrie smiled. He was a perfect weapon, but Shane had something he didn't. Shane had tucked the grief and revenge and hatred away. Now all he had was calm purpose. That was what he needed to get the edge.

It took everything he had not to lose it when Shane screamed. Because at that moment, Reed would've ripped his goddamned arms off to stop the man from calling trouble onto himself. He knew Keith would figure out where they were—Guthrie hadn't taken them far at all. Reed would bet they were in one of the abandoned houses set for foreclosure. Most of the real estate agents and the banks didn't even bother dealing with them until after first thaw.

Guthrie had had a couple of months to plan this.

His neck ached where the dart had hit. His head throbbed. But hell, he was more clearheaded than he'd been in his life.

He could move, but he didn't. Because if Shane could save him, it might make up for more than he realized. So even though the claustrophobia threatened to drown him, he stayed as still as possible and let the man he'd grown to love fight for him, for Kyle, for all of them.

"How would he have known what Reed went through?" Keith demanded as he stared into the TV monitor in Shane's cell. It was the window they could get closest too without setting off alarms. Prophet had disabled a wire or two in order to get them this far. "How does he get his intel?"

"That mission was classified." Prophet's eyes were stony, his demeanor way too calm, the way it always was whenever that particular mission was referenced.

Now, they waited, eyes on the fight and on Reed. Both men strained at the bit to go in and save Reed, but for Shane, they held off.

"If he fucks this up, I'll kill him myself," Prophet promised.

"He won't." Keith shifted between watching the box and watching Shane fight. He'd been right—Shane had been holding back during their sessions. Granted, he'd been recovering as well, but Keith would've recognized these moves instantly.

But Guthrie was no slouch, and this fight was well matched. Both men were staggering and more than a little bloody. To his credit, Shane had yet to use the knife. This was a knock-down, drag-out, bare-knuckles brawl. A fight to the death.

"We can't let him kill Guthrie."

"The fuck we can't," Prophet huffed. "Kill the bastard myself if I have to."

"Just call your CIA contacts and let them know what's happening."

"Why?"

"Maybe Shane wants his old job back."

Prophet shook his head as if to say why would anyone be that stupid, but he walked away and made a call. Keith remained rooted to the spot, ready to move if Shane needed him.

He was fighting for Kyle. For Reed. Most of all, he was fighting for himself— because he was whole again now, and no one would ever take that away from him.

Guthrie's mouth was bleeding, but he still wore that grin, the one he'd always used when he was sparring. Shane would wipe it right off. He did a roundhouse kick that caught Guthrie behind his knee. Then, a hand to the back of the neck and he brought his knee up and heard the snap and the scream as he broke Guthrie's nose.

Yeah, no more smiling now.

He backed up as Guthrie stumbled away. Before the man straightened, Shane ran for him, ramming his head into the man's midsection, slamming him against the wall with a hard thud. As Guthrie began sliding down the wall, he grabbed the man's hair and hit his head against the wall. Once, twice and Guthrie slumped intounconsciousness.

He yanked the knife out of its sheath and grabbed Guthrie by the hair on top of his head, exposing his neck. Killing him would be the eye for an eye, bring the greatest satisfaction, and for a long moment he almost didn't stop himself.

He won't suffer this way. And that's what stopped Shane. Instead, he put the knife down, opened the door for Keith, who came around the corner. Shane didn't wait; instead he opened the door of the second locked cell-like room and went to the box.

He undid the heavy lock and opened it, saying, "Reed, it's me. You're okay.

We're safe—Keith is here."

Reed was staring straight ahead. It had obviously taken all of his strength and concentration not to panic, and he hadn't.

Shane could tell, because the skin on the man's wrists was intact. Reed stared up at him. Blinked a few times. And then he smiled. "You did good, kid," he managed, his voice hoarse, and then Shane was helping him up and out of the box.

"You did too," Shane told him. "And fuck, I wish you hadn't had to."

"Stop. I feel like I got a second chance. A way to get rid of the nightmares.

And I think you did too."

"Because of Keith."

"He's never going to let us live this down."

"And we're lucky as hell for it."

When they walked back out of the room, Reed's arms around Shane's neck, they found Prophet holding Keith's knife and Guthrie dead on the floor. There was something in Prophet's eyes that made Shane not say a word, just allowed the man to come on the other side of Reed and bring them outside into Keith's waiting truck.

EPILOGUE

Six months later

Shane stretched as he stood in the middle of the jet, not yet awake.

"Par for the course," Keith mumbled as he glanced up at him. Shane blinked a few times and looked around to get his bearings.

Right—the jet. Executive Enterprises, LTD. The mission. Keith. Reed.

He pulled the thin blanket tighter around his shoulders and grinned. "Yeah, he's back," Reed said with a chuckle.

"How're your ribs?" Keith asked.

Shane frowned, moved the blanket and tried to look at his side that was bruised up from the recent mission, ended up turning around in a circle like a dog chasing his tail. "Shit, you did that on purpose."

Keith and Reed were laughing too hard to say anything. "That's not fair to do to a wounded man," he protested.

"I'm going to do a lot more unfair things to you when we get home. Both of you," Keith announced.

"Not if I do them to both of you first," Shane echoed.

"I told you, he's a bad influence," Keith said, but he looked anything but unhappy, especially when Reed nodded enthusiastically. "Now sit down and buckle up. Gary's prepping to land."

He'd just returned from his first mission with both men. The feeling possessing him now was heady. It had been a relief to be in the field again, to show off his confidence.

A relief to be able to come back to the cabin with both men and call it home.

The CIA had offered him his old job, which meant he'd be going back to undercover work. When he'd refused, they'd given him a great pension as a shut-up gift. Guthrie was dead, because that's how the CIA takes care of their own, Prophet said darkly. And even though Shane knew Prophet was right, Shane couldn't figure out if Prophet thought that was a good thing or not.

All Shane knew was that somehow, Kyle had a hand in leading him down the right path to where he belonged.

NEWSLETTER

Sign up for the newsletter of SE Jakes and her alter-ego Stephanie Tyler!

Be among the first to learn not only about new and upcoming books but also appearances and signings as well as special promotions and giveaways!

http://stephanietyler.com/newsletter/

NOW AVAILABLE:

BOUND TO BREAK

MEN OF HONOR

TURN THE PAGE TO READ MORE...

MEN OF HONOR, BOOK 6

Four men fighting against their pasts...and for each other.

Several years after washing up on a beach in South Africa with absolutely no memory—not even his name—Lucky would rather *not* remember his past. Based on the number of scars on his body, it couldn't have been anything good.

Then a man claiming to be his former Navy SEAL teammate walks into the bar and insists that Lucky's real name is Josiah Joshua Kent. Turns out he's been listed as KIA, and since he's not dead, he's now considered a deserter.

Discovering Josh is alive throws Rex, and his relationship with Sawyer, into a tailspin. Rex can finally lay to rest the nightmares of the night he couldn't save his teammate. And Sawyer is faced with his *worst* nightmare—a relationship threatened by a very real ghost from the past.

As Josh begins to piece his memories back together, another man with a shadowy connection to his past—and maybe his heart—holds the key that could free him. Or send him to a traitor's fate.

Warning: Contains rough language, rougher sex and warriors who fall hard for one another.

PROLOGUE

It was too dark to see, the air so humid it threatened to drown him in the enclosed space. His head throbbed, his body had gone numb weeks ago. And there was no end in sight.

He couldn't stand—the cell was maybe four feet tall and eight feet wide, at best, and the claustrophobia closed in on him minute by minute, so much so that he'd started to look forward to the beatings because at least he was freed then. And upright, strapped to a T-bar while he was whipped, questions screamed at him in between that he never goddamned answered.

You don't know how much you can handle until you're forced to handle it.

That statement had too much truth to it. Especially when his captors dangled the eternal carrot in front of him and his teammates, day in and day out.

"If you help us, your friends can go."

Night after night, he pondered the truth in that statement when he knew there really was none. But lack of food and sleep did strange things to a man, and no amount of training could've ever thoroughly prepared him for this.

For this kind of torture, you were either able to make it through or you weren't. Simple as that. It was a mental game…unless your body broke down physically. After that, all bets were off.

None of them wanted to scream but sometimes the screams slipped out. He'd listen for other signs of suffering—the fast breathing, the grunts that came out involuntarily after being hit too hard.

The terrorists with ties to the FARC were looking for the same intel they'd killed a CIA agent for—wanted a terrorist released from prison in exchange for the second agent's life. He knew that because his team had been sent in to rescue that agent.

There was no sign of the agent, not before or after the SEAL team had been captured.

"You'll cooperate."

He looked up, stared into the face of his captor. "You will cooperate."

"No," he managed.

"One of your friends is already dead because you wouldn't cooperate."

He couldn't answer that. Wouldn't. He was dragged out, but far less roughly. His head spun. His body was too weak, and the men half carried him into a small room he'd never been let into before. And they hadn't taken him past his teammates' cells this time.

He had no idea if they were getting out of this alive. He did know that if they did, they'd never be the same.

1

There were a lot of people looking to get laid in the packed bar that night, and Lucky wanted to be one of them. The lights were low, music screamed in his ears and his body moved unconsciously to the beat as he poured drinks and flirted easily with the regulars.

Emme waved him down. "Luck, give me four lemon-drop shots." Emme always called him Luck, short for Lucky, because she'd been the one to name him that after finding him washed up on the beach in the middle of the night.

"I tripped over you and I screamed," Emme told him all the time. "First, I thought it was a dead whale. And then I thought you were just dead."

I was, he always thought when she told that part.

Dead and reborn Lucky on that wet sand on the Easter Cape beach almost four years earlier. He didn't even know how old he was. Didn't know his real name, if his parents were dead or alive.

But the scars that striped across his back and the backs of his thighs told him he'd been through a terrible ordeal. He'd incorporated that into his made-up past, told the doctors and Emme's family—the Bains—that his name was Doug, that he'd been abused as a teen and that he'd emancipated himself and was traveling, doing odd jobs and determined to live life on his terms.

The last part was true enough. He'd told the Bains that he'd gone out too far and the riptide had yanked him.

The thing was, the riptide *had* been there, but he'd instinctively known to swim along with it, parallel to the shore instead of trying to fight it. This was where his memory started—a terrifying moment of waking up submerged in the dark water. He'd been lucky he hadn't inhaled, which spoke of luck.

Or maybe experience.

He'd discovered he knew how to swim seconds after being dumped into the Indian Ocean that night. And he had swum—it had been more sophisticated than panicked survival instinct. Because he hadn't panicked. He'd been exhausted but he'd finally found a place where the current broke and had swum until he hit sand. He'd lain on the beach, freezing, until the Bains had found him. His first instinct on meeting Emme and her parents had been to lie. That had worked out well for him, and he'd remained in South Africa ever since.

He was most likely American, but had no passport, no social security number to prove that, so leaving wasn't on his highest list of priorities. And this pace of life had suited him, at least at first.

Lately, he'd been restless. He guessed having no choices would do that to a man eventually.

"Here you go." He slid the shots down the bar, one by one toward the waiting women. They laughed as they caught the glasses and thanked him. One, a tall, pretty brunette, held up her shot and toasted him before moving to be closer to where he was working. She flirted with him for a few minutes—he returned the banter but he was too busy for anything more.

That was all right—she wasn't his type anyway. "Hey, can I grab a Jack and Coke?"

Lucky looked up into the face of the man who'd placed the order and nodded. "Coming right up."

The guy did a double take. He was good-looking, but Lucky had immediately pegged him for straight. He waited a beat, but the guy suddenly reached across the bar for him, saying, "Josh? Holy fuck—is that really you?"

Lucky put his hands up and backed away.

The name Josh didn't set off any alarm bells, but Lucky would be lying if he hadn't thought about a moment like this constantly. Some days he looked over his shoulder more than others.

Tonight, his defenses had been down. His gut told him to move this away from the bar, take it outside so Emme wouldn't see it happening. He pushed out, calling, "Taking ten," and didn't wait to hear her agree.

The big blond guy followed him. When Lucky turned to face him under the lights in the adjacent alleyway, he noted the guy looked like he'd seen a ghost. "How the hell did you escape?"

"I'm not Josh," he said.

"You're Josh Kent. Come on, I'd know you anywhere," the guy started again, softer this time, like one might talk to a wounded animal. He kept his hands to himself, tucked them into his jeans pockets to make himself appear less threatening.

But Lucky was threatened. Half of him fought a tremble but the other half was ready to throw down. Instinct made him react, forced him to keep a wide berth between the two of them. "You've got the wrong guy."

But he persisted. "Josh, it's Nate. We served together."

Fuck. Served together. He'd long suspected he'd been in the military, but he played dumb instead, hoping it was all a case of mistaken identity. "Served drinks?"

"In the Navy."

"My name's Lucky, not Josh. Sorry." He went to turn away but Nate grabbed his upper arm forcefully and spun him around.

"Four years, Josh. We all thought you died. We watched you…fuck…we watched you die and now you're hanging out bartending?" Nate let go of him, put his hands up as if apologizing. "If you don't remember…"

"I don't know what you're talking about." Lucky pushed

at him, his palms against the big guy's shoulders, and Nate stumbled back.

"Strong as ever, you dumb fuck. Why the hell are you hiding here?"

"You need to leave," Lucky said, but Nate was charging for him, angry now. He braced but Nate stopped when another man stepped in between them.

That guy was also big and broad, and for a horrible second, Lucky thought he was on Nate's side. But he put himself in front of Lucky and told Nate, "You need to back off."

"You don't understand—I know him," Nate said.

"He doesn't know you. He's said so. Chalk it up to a case of mistaken identity."

"It's not," Nate insisted. "I'll leave now—but I'll be back with proof. You're Josh Kent." He pointed at Lucky and then stormed off.

Lucky walked over to the nearest car and sat on the hood. Sweat trickled down his back and he took a deep breath. He'd built a web of lies about who he was. All this time, he hadn't told anyone he couldn't remember shit about his past. And really, how would they know?

He didn't tell them because they'd make him deal with it, and he was pretty damned sure he didn't want to go there again. Ever.

"He scared the hell out of you," his savior said, his voice rough. So was his hand that reached out to touch him, but the good rough that made Lucky feel something. The calming hand rested on the back of his neck, centered him, allowed him to simply bow his head and take a deep breath.

The hand remained there for what seemed like hours but was really just minutes. He finally raised his head and the guy's hand slid off.

Lucky missed the contact. "I'm okay. I've been fighting a flu," he lied, because that's apparently what he did best. "Thanks for that—I just wasn't up to dealing with a stalker."

"Is that what he was?"

He looked into the pale blue eyes that seemed to want truth and barely managed, "Yeah."

"Well, any employee of my family's bar is typically like family." He blinked. "You're Dashiell."

"Dash."

In all these years, he'd never met Emme's brother, an award-winning photographer. Emme said he always avoided being photographed himself, just let his work speak for him. There were a lot of his prints around Lucky's apartment, haunting pictures of people and places in third-world countries. Lucky was always drawn to them as though he'd been there, looking over his shoulder as the pictures were taken. Like he had a connection to Dash, which was ridiculous.

"I've seen your photographs. Great stuff." He sounded like an idiot. Blamed Nate for riling him up and tried to calm down. "Emme always brags about you."

"She's good for that," Dash agreed. He wore his blond hair long, tied back. The stubble on his face looked like it would be rough too if Lucky rubbed his hand against it. There was a scar on his chin that Lucky wanted to trace down to his neck. Looked dressed down, like he'd blend in anywhere. But he was just handsome enough to be memorable.

Lucky didn't know why he did that—catalogued people quickly, studied, looking and assessing for strengths and weaknesses—but he did it all the damned time.

You were in the Navy.

"Speaking of Emme, I need to get back in there." Lucky slid off the car, and Dash put a hand on his shoulder, as if to steady him. Whether he'd needed it or not, he liked the way it felt.

Dash walked into his family's bar a step behind Lucky, tamping down the adrenaline that threatened to take over his body. For a second before he entered, he closed his eyes and mentally compared the old picture from the file to the man he'd had his hands on.

It was hard not to reach out and touch the guy again, and he cursed himself for even doing so in the first place. It wasn't the reaction he'd pictured having when he'd finally been proven correct in believing that Josh Kent—aka "Lucky"—was alive.

Alive, with a possible terrorist connection and living with your family.

Lucky didn't even turn around after he jumped behind the bar and began taking drink orders. Emme went to say something to him but spotted Dash and ran over to him instead. He noted that Lucky looked relieved. "Finally! I was beginning to think you'd disowned us."

He hugged her back. "Sorry—work's been keeping me busy."

"I know. I collect your work, remember?" She swatted him with the towel she'd had tucked in her jeans and they walked to the back room where it was quieter. "Please tell me you're sticking around for a little while."

"At least a couple of days."

"I see you met our best bartender." She motioned over her shoulder at Lucky.

He took a deep breath and held back, because scaring the shit out of his sister—or letting Lucky know he was suspicious—was the last thing Dash wanted to do. "Yep. Lucky's an unusual first name."

"It's a nickname—we gave it to him when we rescued him."

Dash crossed his arms and waited for the story. "Okay, not so much rescued him, because he was fine, but he'd been swimming and he'd fallen asleep on the beach and he was freezing."

"And so you and Mom and Dad decided to add him to

the family tree?"

"We took him to hospital when we couldn't wake him up. He didn't have any ID on him and he looked like…" She shook her head, stopped her train of thought. "Anyway, he's a good guy. Helps with stuff around the bar and the house too. Never missed work. He's honest and the customers love him."

Dash could see that. Lucky was a tall, good-looking guy. His dark hair was done in a messy fashion—not too long, not too short. Good hair. Serious dark-brown eyes.

Dash had seen Lucky struggling with his anger when Nate questioned him, had watched him flex his hands as though unconsciously preparing for hand-to-hand combat.

He'd had the right stance for it. Even if he hadn't known who Lucky really was, Dash would've said he was no goddamned bartender…not until he'd backed off and acted like he was on the verge of a panic attack.

It was like he'd been fighting a part of himself. "He's using the apartment," Emme continued. "My apartment?"

"You haven't been home in six years."

"But I'm here now." He blew out a frustrated breath.

There was definitely something going on with Lucky, but the guy had been here for four years and he'd done nothing. He was staying in Dash's apartment—he knew who Dash was. Four years and he hadn't made his move. It didn't make sense.

Dash's family had to pay Lucky in cash, unless he'd had

the means to get a fake ID and start a bank account. But if he had an ID, why stay in one place for four years? Why not hide?

Unless he'd decided on hiding in plain sight.

Dash had been in these circles too long not to notice when something wasn't right. Obviously, his family hadn't inherited any of his situational awareness, but they were used to *him* being suspicious. Emme always attributed it to him working in some of the world's most dangerous places, and she was right. But she only knew half his truth. His photography was a convenient cover story for his other work, the kind you could never tell family about without putting them at risk.

He'd stayed away so he wouldn't do that. And now, he discovered that his family had invited a risk to live and work with them. A man Dash had been searching for.

You've got the wrong guy.

He'd never thought this moment would actually come, not like this, with a man who appeared to have no memory of who he was. Dash had been the only one to believe Josh Kent might be alive. Sometimes, being right wasn't all it was cracked up to be.

"You can stay at the house," Emme told him.

No way. "I'll talk to Lucky. Maybe he'll let me crash in the extra room for a few nights."

Emme's face was unreadable, but all she said was, "It's closing time—I've got to do last call. Then we'll talk more."

Yes, they would.

He watched Lucky and Emme interact. Lucky was still shaken—he couldn't hide that—but there was an easy chemistry between him and Emme that was plain as day. Lucky was protective of her, and in turn, she made him smile. There was a rhythm between the two of them behind the bar that spoke of long nights working together, a closeness that Dash himself didn't have with his sister any longer.

Unable to shake off the melancholy that mixed in with the unease, he tore his eyes away from Lucky and looked around the old place. He guessed it was true that the more things changed, the more they stayed the same. The bar was in a perfect spot to attract all the locals but just upscale enough to keep the tourists pouring in. Most were dressed casually, some still in cover-ups over their bathing suits.

Last call was more raucous than usual. Dash was glad. It allowed him to slip out again and wait in the parking lot for Nate.

Nate, whom he'd been tracking for the past four years, because he traveled the most out of the three SEALs who'd returned home after the capture. He wasn't disappointed. He'd been outside maybe five minutes when the guy was back, storming across the dusty parking area. When he saw Dash, he stopped short, then motioned for Dash to come with him around the side of the bar.

This was the first time Dash had actually gotten on a

plane and followed him. That was because he'd made plans to come to Dash's hometown, his family.

Yes, Nate surfed all over the world, and this beach was a well-known surfing spot. But for Dash, he couldn't risk it simply being a coincidence—not with his family involved.

"How well do you know Lucky?" Nate asked without preamble. "I don't."

"I do." Nate handed him his phone and Dash paged through several photos. Lucky, standing next to Nate, in jungle BDUs. Lucky, hugging a guy with a shaved head, looking happy. "That's Rex. He and Josh lived together."

"Did you tell him anything?"

Nate's expression tightened. "It would kill him if I'm wrong. It'll kill him anyway."

"Unless Josh Kent has a twin…" Dash trailed off.

"I worked with him for years. I know who that is—I'd know him anywhere." Nate paused. "We thought we lost him on a mission four years ago."

"Torture?"

Nate nodded. "I saw him die."

"Scars?"

Nate lifted his chin. "We were captured. Tortured. He was killed. Burned."

"Guessing it wasn't him."

"Obviously. We never looked for a body because we all saw it burn."

"So he might've been tortured for as long as you guys.

Maybe longer. Escaped. Lost his memory along the way."

"Check him for scars—lots of them. Like this." Nate turned, lifted his shirt and showed broad stripes that would never heal. "They'd be on the backs of his thighs too. And he's burned. His lower back, below the waistline. Plus a scar on his calf." He lowered his shirt and turned back.

"You're retired?"

"Yes."

Nate had retired willingly. Whether he passed psych evals or not wasn't disclosed. Uncle was another SEAL on that team who'd been forced into retirement after a long medical leave because his arms hadn't healed right from the torture he'd been put through. Rex was still active duty with an impeccable record.

"How'd you end up here?"

"I end up in a lot of places," was all Nate said. "What do you do for a living?"

"I'm just a photographer."

"Right." Nate drew out the word. "Look, I know you're going to check me and my story out. Not sure why the hell you're here, if it's dumb luck or if you know about Josh. Either way, our kind recognizes our kind. Don't fuck with me."

Dash shrugged, and for Nate, he guessed that was enough of an answer. The guy might've thought he was a merc too, or retired military or something along those lines, and he'd be damned close to the truth. "Let me feel him out. If he's a lost POW, he needs to deal with it."

Nate nodded. "I've got to report this to the Navy. This is a big goddamned deal. He has classified intel."

Not if he doesn't have a memory. "Give me twenty-four hours."

"What are you going to do?"

"See if I can figure out if he's for real or if he's a deserter. He's been living and working with my family."

"The Josh I knew was a good guy."

"People change," Dash said.

ALSO BY SE JAKES

Men of Honor Series
BOUND BY HONOR
BOUND BY LAW
TIES THAT BIND
BOUND BY DANGER
BOUND FOR KEEPS
BOUND TO BREAK

Phoenix, Inc. Series
NO BOUNDARIES

Inked Series
HOLD THE LINE
THIRDS

EE LTD. Universe
FREE FALLING

Hell or High Water Series
CATCH A GHOST
LONG TIME GONE
DAYLIGHT AGAIN
NOT FADE AWAY
IF I EVER

Dirty Deeds Series
DIRTY DEEDS

Havoc MC Series
RUNNING WILD
RUNNING BLIND

Bluewater Bay (multi-author series)
NO EASY WAY (novella) in the *LIGHTS, CAMERA, ACTION* Anthology

WRITING AS STEPHANIE TYLER

Shelter Series
SHELTER ME
PIECES OF ME (coming Fall 2016)

Mirror Series
MIRROR ME
RULE OF THIRDS
WALK IN MY SHADOW
DOUBLE BLIND (coming 2017)

Skulls Creek MC Series
VIPERS RUN
VIPERS RULE

Section 8 Series
SURRENDER
UNBREAKABLE

FRAGMENTED
Defiance Series
DEFIANCE
REDEMPTION
SALVATION
TEMPERANCE

Dire Wolves Series
DIRE WARNING (prequel novella)
DIRE NEEDS
DIRE WANTS
DIRE DESIRES

Shadow Force Series
LIE WITH ME
PROMISES IN THE DARK
IN THE AIR TONIGHT
NIGHT MOVES
LONELY IS THE NIGHT

Hold Series
HARD TO HOLD
TOO HOT TO HOLD
HOLD ON TIGHT
HOLDING ON (novella)

Hot Nights, Dark Desires Anthology
NIGHT VISION (novella)

Harlequin Blaze
COMING UNDONE
RISKING IT ALL
BEYOND HIS CONTROL

WRITING AS SYDNEY CROFT

ACRO Series
RIDING THE STORM
UNLEASHING THE STORM
SEDUCED BY THE STORM
TAMING THE FIRE
TEMPTING THE FIRE
TAKEN BY FIRE
THREE THE HARD WAy (novella)

Hot Nights, Dark Desires Anthology
SHADOW PLAY (novella)

ABOUT THE AUTHOR

SE JAKES is the pen name for *New York Times* bestselling author Stephanie Tyler, and half the co-writing team of Sydney Croft. First published in 2011, SE Jakes has quickly risen to be a bestselling author in the LGBT romance genre, as well as a fan favorite. Her books are frequently highlighted in *USA Today* and have been reviewed by *Library Journal* and *RT Books Magazine*. She's been nominated by several sites for Favorite M/M author and has finaled in the Goodreads M/M Romance Readers Choice Awards in 7 categories. She's a hybrid author who writes for Riptide Publishing and Samhain Publishing, and she indie publishes as well.

STEPHANIE TYLER is the *New York Times* bestselling author of romance novels spanning multiple genres, including Romantic Suspense, New Adult, Paranormal Romance and Contemporary Romance. She's a hybrid author who writes for multiple publishers, including Random House, NAL/Penguin, Harlequin, Carina Press, Mammoth Books, Belle Books and Samhain Publishing, as well as Riptide (as SE Jakes) and indie publishing. Her books have been translated into half a dozen languages, nominated for an RT Readers' Choice Award and garnered top picks from *RT Book Magazine* as well as starred reviews from *Publishers Weekly*. She's a frequent workshop presenter and has contributed stories for anthologies for charities, including **SEAL of My Dreams**, which has raised over 150K for the Veterans Medical Association.

SYDNEY CROFT is the alter ego of Stephanie Tyler and Larissa Ione, two *New York Times* bestselling authors who blend their very different writing interests into adventurous tales of erotic paranormal fiction. Together, they developed a world where people with extraordinary abilities, like the power to control storms, could live and work with others like them. The series has been described as "Erotica meets the X-Men," and is unique in its own "erotic superhero romance" niche. Larissa and Stephanie live in different states and communicate almost entirely through email, though they often get together for conferences and book signings.